THE DREAMFIGHTER
AND OTHER CREATION TALES

The Dreamfighter and Other Creation Tales

TED HUGHES

faber and faber

First published in Great Britain in 1995
by Faber and Faber Limited
3 Queen Square London WC1N 3AU
in association with Jackanory

Typeset by Wilmaset Ltd, Wirral
Printed in England by Clays Ltd, St Ives plc

© Ted Hughes, 1995

Ted Hughes is hereby identified as author of this
work in accordance with Section 77 of the Copyright,
Designs and Patents Act 1988

A CIP record for this book
is available from the British Library

ISBN 0–571–17566–X

009914

2 4 6 8 10 9 7 5 3 2 1

for Carol

Contents

Goku

Right in the beginning, when everything was being made, God worked night and day, and his helpers were the Angels and the Demons. His Angels made the insides of things. His Demons made the outsides. God told them how it should be done and they did it. They were tireless workers.

But one of the Demons was different. His name was Goku. Goku would not work. Or rather, he would work only in his own way. He worked in such a clownish way, all the other Demons laughed, sometimes so hard that they had to stop work, which made God angry.

Here is the sort of thing Goku did. When they were making the river Amazon, God had given his instructions. And the Angels had made a gigantic River Spirit. This was the inside part of the river Amazon. God was pleased. It was one of his masterpieces. From one angle it looked like an enormous Indian woman lying across the landscape, naked and draped only with flower garlands, beside a full-length mirror, admiring herself as she combed her hair. From another angle, it looked like a colossal snake, looped and coiled across the map, with a huge great-lipped mouth resting on the edge of the sea, into which it sang gloomy songs. Every one of its scales was like a lens, and when you looked into one of those lenses you saw a fish, or a crab, or an insect, or a bird, or a reptile peering out, as if it were hiding inside the lens.

From another angle the River Spirit looked like a horde of ragged goblins, pouring towards the sea. Every one of them was monstrous, and every one different. Imagine for yourself. Some were luminous, and were half frog, half monkey. Some bounded along on a single leg, with the bone sharpened to a point. Some were simply heads, happily or unhappily rolling. And so on. The hubbub was deafening. Their wagons, loaded with magic drums, flutes, fishing tackle, looms and cooking pots, trundled along with them, pulled by alligators, tapirs, jaguars and wild pigs.

From another angle, it was nothing but an old man, trudging along. Just one lonely old man. Yet wherever you looked, along the whole length of the river, there he was, trudging along, the same old man.

From every angle it appeared to be something different.

This was the inside of the river, the River Spirit, made by the Angels.

When the Demons started making the outside of the river, they had a problem. They had to invent an endless supply of water. Plain, ordinary water. They all thought hard how to do it.

Then Goku cried: 'I've got it!'

He grabbed the River Spirit, tied a mountain range round its neck, and threw this huge weight out into the middle of the Atlantic Ocean. The whole River Spirit flew through the air like a long streamer tied to a cannonball. As it disappeared under the Atlantic, Goku let out his laugh. He really had thought it was a good idea. He had plunged the River Spirit into endless water, just as God had wanted. But now he saw how alarming his solution was. And how wrong. And how funny.

The Demons lay laughing helplessly all around him. The Angels rushed to rescue the River Spirit before it perished in the salt water, and God was furious. But Goku only said: 'You told us it needed water. Now it's got it.'

When God invented Man, it was just the same. This was quite a tricky job, especially when it came to making the head. The Angels had made the inside of Man's head – the Head Spirit, thinking brilliant thoughts, planning a happy future, solving every problem, and dreaming of songs.

But then the Demons had to make the outside. They sat in thought, wrinkling their demon brows. Suddenly Goku cried: 'I've got it!'

He pulled up a turnip, which God had invented a few days before, and stuck it on Man's shoulders. 'There,' he said. 'Two birds with one stone.'

But then when he saw what he'd done he laughed so hard all the Demons laughed with him, rolling up and down Heaven, the Earth and the Underworld. They thought it was very funny. But the Angels frowned. The part of God that was black went white with rage. And the part that was white went black.

Man did look very odd with a leafy turnip for a head. But God's rage frightened Goku. 'I'll fix it,' cried the Demon. And with quick scoops and gougings of his demon claws, he carved the turnip into a face.

'What's wrong with that?' he asked. But then when he saw what his claws had done, he let out his wild ear-splitting laugh.

God threw down his book of ideas and went storming off into a far corner of Heaven. He thought he might explode and annihilate his own Creation. He really did feel dangerous. Even the Angels were frightened.

Quickly, before God came back, the Angels made the inside of Woman. And this time, before Goku could spoil things with one of his crazy ideas, the Demons gave Woman's head and face a beautiful outside, just like the most beautiful of the Demons. And before God came back, Man and Woman had two children, Boy and Girl – but their heads were half turnip, just as they are to this day. It was too late for God to correct. After that, whenever Goku saw Man or one of his children he let out his awful laugh. God began to dread the sound of it.

And so God planned how to get rid of Goku.

But just at that moment Goku found another Demon exactly like himself. A female Demon named Goka. He recognized her on sight as one of his own kind and she recognized him. They stared at each other with joyful faces and let out a fierce wild laugh that ripped the paint off God's toy motor car, which he was saving up to give to Man when the right moment came.

Goka was almost crazier than Goku. 'Where have you been all these billions of years?' cried Goku, gazing at her in rapture.

'I've been up my mother's nostril, plugged in with a poggle,' she explained, and let out her loopy wild laugh.

Whatever they said to each other, they followed it with a laugh. The Demons grinned, waiting for what amusing thing they would do next. But the Angels watched sternly.

'One day,' said Goka, 'I'll make those Angels laugh so hard their jaws will break off. They'll laugh so hard they'll be treading on their tongues. They'll laugh so hard their eyes will come bouncing off the wall. They'll laugh so hard their hearts will be jumping about on their plates – '

Goku silenced her with a kiss.

'Let's do it together, my love,' he said.

So she and Goku set out to make the Angels laugh.

They almost brought Creation to a standstill. God was inventing new things all the time, and the Angels, as ever, were making angelic insides for them. But when it came to the turn of the Demons to make the outsides – Goku and Goka were there, making trouble.

That is how so many things came to be made wrong.

Suddenly God had a brainwave. If Goka has a baby, he thought, she will calm down. She'll become sensible. And Goku too, he will become serious. Fathers become serious.

God gave a quiet little laugh – and there was Goka, about to have a baby. She burst into tears. Goku licked his lips, scratched his head, then got up and walked to and fro, uttering a wild laugh. Then he sat down again and frowned.

Suddenly Goka jumped up. 'I've got it!' she cried. 'I know what!'

She flew down to Woman and whispered in her ear: 'You are going to have God's child.'

Woman, who was dozing on her veranda, woke with a start. She told Man. 'An Angel just came,' she said. 'It told me I'm going to have God's child.'

'Are you sure it was an Angel?' Man asked. He knew something about the Demons.

'It was made of light,' Woman said. 'It had fierce eyes.'

Man also knew something about the Angels. He knew they were made of light. The Demons were made of darkness.

His eyes grew round, gazing at his wife. 'An Angel!' he whispered.

'It looked exactly like me,' she added.

Man's eyes narrowed. How angelic was his wife?

Next day, there was the Babe in its cradle.

'My little darling!' cried Woman.

'Can this be God's child?' whispered Man.

The Babe looked at them with bright eyes like a bird, and let out a wild, unearthly laugh.

When God saw what Goka had done with her baby, he shook his head. 'Just like a Demon!' he exclaimed. The time had come to do something drastic about her and her mad husband. He called to the Demons to heat his furnace white-hot, and he rolled up his sleeves. Then he bound Goku and Goka together, face to face, with heavenly wire, and heated them white-hot in the furnace. Then, laying them on his anvil, he pounded them with his mighty hammer till the sparks flew.

Again he heated them white-hot, and again he pounded them on the anvil, gripping them with his pincers as his almighty arm rose and fell, and the hammer blows shook Heaven and Earth.

Goku and Goka no longer laughed. Their faces were squeezed into one face, their bodies into one body, as God hammered them into a single lump.

Again he heated them white-hot, and again he hammered them. And as he hammered, the lump grew smaller. And smaller. Till it was only the size of a thrush's egg.

Then he plunged it into icy water, with a bang of steam.

He took it out, and rolled it between his palms. In spite of the icy dip, it was warm and dry. He gave it to an Angel. 'Take this,' he said, 'and give it to any bird who will take it.'

So the Angel came down to Earth, where the birds were singing. He called them together and explained that God had invented a new egg. He showed them the ball. 'So which of you will take it and hatch it and nurse what comes out?'

The birds were silent. But finally the Hedge Sparrow piped up: 'If it's God's,' she said, 'then I'll take it.' And she put it with her own five eggs.

Out of that egg two chicks hatched. They screamed to be fed. And screamed. And screamed. They took all the food their parents brought. And they grew.

They tossed the Hedge Sparrow's own children out of the nest. And screamed to be fed.

'Are these truly God's?' asked the male Hedge Sparrow. His head was worn bare with pushing food down the throats of these two gaping mouths.

One day, the two strange creatures flew up and away.

They began to fly to and fro over the Earth. One was male, one female. She called 'Goku!' and he called 'Goka!'

When she lays an egg, she does what she did before, and what the Angel did. She gives it to somebody else. She finds Hedge Sparrow's nest, and pops it in, and flies off with a weird laugh.

They ignore the other birds. They try to attract the attention of the Angels, and of the Demons, that stream to and fro in the air invisibly, going about God's business.

'Goku!' they cry, and 'Goka!' at the tops of their voices, all day long. And as the days pass, they grow more and more desperate. They turn somersaults. They shout their names and follow that with a mad demonic laugh, hoping they will be recognized.

But the Angels and the Demons are still too busy. And God refuses to take any notice. Only Man listens. He pauses, and listens. And as he listens to that endless 'Goku!' and 'Goka!', and now and then that laugh echoing between the woods, a strange feeling comes over him. He feels he wants to laugh madly. He feels something is missing – something very important. And he feels the Angels watching him sternly.

The Dreamfighter

God was in a bad way. The trouble was – things from outer space. These alien beings would land at night, dress themselves in nightmare, and creep into his ear.

His sleep was gone. The only way he could escape the attacks of these ferocious beings was to stay awake. So night after night he paced to and fro in his workshop. Sometimes, for sheer weariness, he would sit. But then if he closed his eyes, even for a moment, his head would loll forward and he would be asleep.

And a nightmare would creep into his ear.

He'd stopped doing any real work, creating real creatures. He made a few plants. Doodling with clay, he made a few kinds of fly. But his heart wasn't in it. The truth was, he felt too sleepy.

One afternoon sleep was weighing heavy on him. Struggling to keep awake, he began to doodle with clay. And this time, yawning, rubbing his eyelids that kept trying to stick together, and almost dreaming with his eyes open, he made an odd thing.

It was red, with red eyes. About the size of an Alsatian dog. Six skinny legs. It waved two feelers.

And it stared at him. And it cried: 'What am I?'

God stared back. He had simply no idea what it was, or what to call it. Usually when he made a creature he had a pretty strong picture of what he wanted and why he wanted it. But this time his mind was blank.

'What am I?' it cried again, shivering.

God scratched his head and yawned. He supposed he ought to give it a name.

'Tell me what I am,' cried the creature. 'Tell me what I have to do.'

But God's head had already fallen forward, and a snore came out of his beard.

The creature blinked its red eyes and strayed into the forest.

For a long time, it simply stood under a tree. Other creatures going busily past looked sideways at it and said: 'A new one! What are you?'

But the creature didn't know what to say.

A Baboon marched past. 'Haha!' it barked. 'A new-comer! Name please.'

When the creature didn't answer, Baboon gave it a shove, and it collapsed like an ironing board. It got up slowly.

'Can't you speak?' asked the Baboon. 'Then you must be a Mutant. Get it? Mute Ant. Hahaha!' And the Baboon rolled over backwards, beating its head with mirth. It ran off to tell some Gazelles.

'Mutant?' thought the creature. 'Well, maybe I am. Maybe the Monkey's right.'

But that didn't help. He still didn't know what to do.

And the trouble was, he didn't feel like doing anything either.

The Cheetah hurtled past, along the trail of dust left by a Gerenuk, and he heard its claws hissing: 'Faster! Faster!' What was the hurry?

A long line of Gnu, heads bowed with effort, climbed away north, grunting: 'North! North!' Where were they all going?

And just above him, two Wrens came and went, came and went, came and went, every half-minute, holding a feather, or a string of moss, or a stalk of grass. Why were they so busy?

He watched some Flamingoes holding their heads upside down, half under water. What were they trying to do?

'If I'm a Mutant,' he thought, 'what does a Mutant do? Why did God make me? I'm not properly made. I don't seem to fit. He must have left something out of my works.'

He walked around, watching the animals and the birds all so busy. 'How do they know what to be busy with?' he thought. He did feel completely left out.

That same day, God advertised for a bodyguard, to defend him from his nightmares. *Must be a good night-worker and dreamfighter*, said his ad. Three creatures had applied: Leopard, Wolf and Owl. God was giving each one a try. Leopard first, then Wolf, then Owl.

But none of them could stand up to the Space Beings.

The first night, Leopard saw two eyes coming closer.

They were very like his own, but much bigger. 'They look like eyes,' thought Leopard, 'but they are probably flying saucers.' He decided to attack. But when he leapt, the moment his feet left the ground he felt suddenly dizzy. When he landed he was spinning like a top. Not only was he spinning like a top, somebody was lashing him with a whip, to keep him spinning. With an extra crack, the whip lifted him out over the forest, and he crashed into a thorn bush. Scrambling out of the thorns, he shot off to his cave.

That night God had a shocking nightmare. He was a Leopard spinning down a plughole. The plughole was too small. So he was having to become very thin, till he was no thicker than his own tail. So he spun down the plughole and came out as an immensely long, twisting Leopard's tail writhing among the stars, which were all quaking with laughter. He woke up shouting, and no wonder.

The Wolf did no better. The Wolf didn't know what had happened to Leopard. He saw two eyes coming closer. He thought it was another Wolf. He went forward warily. It seemed to be another Wolf, very like himself. They touched noses.

As they touched noses, the other breathed in fiercely, with a sudden, whistling, sucking breath. And Wolf felt himself being sucked in and actually turned inside out inside the other Wolf. 'How can this be?' he howled, and his howl, too, was inside out.

Then the other Wolf sneezed, and Wolf shot away into the darkness, once again outside out and inside in, but so terrified that when he landed he went on running till next morning. From this moment he became three times as wary.

But while Wolf was still running, God had a shocking nightmare. He dreamed he was first turned inside out, then blown up like a very big, very tight balloon. And that's how he spent the night, inside out, blown up as a big balloon, bobbing among the freezing, prickling stars.

Owl had the worst time. Owl saw two eyes coming closer. He'd heard what had happened to Leopard and to Wolf, so he wasn't very happy. He was wishing he hadn't taken this work on. But he was brave, and he was thinking: 'I'll attack, and just grab at those eyes. If I can get my hands on his eyes, he'll be helpless.'

So he attacked. But instead of landing with out-stretched, grasping feet on a solid creature's head, as poor Owl expected, he was hit by something springy, light, flat and very tough. It sent him spinning. And then the same thing, with a whiffling whop, hit him again, from the other direction and sent him spinning back. And hit him again from the other direction. And so it went on. And Owl had no idea what was hitting him, or what was going on, except he was being slapped helplessly through the air, first one way then the other, with whacking, whiffling blows.

Making a terrific effort, he flung out his wings and flew straight upwards. He was free. He hurtled home, all his feathers broken and bent. He squeezed himself into the back of his tree hole. He closed his eyes tight. No more bodyguard jobs for him!

Meanwhile God was having an awful nightmare. Two gigantic tennis rackets were batting him to and fro across a net in which the knots were stars. Every sort of shot, lob and whack, slice and volley slam. God spun in the air, or he flashed like a bullet. Sometimes he hit the net and stars showered. Then the racket flipped him up and – Bop! – away he went again. He woke next morning hardly able to move.

After this, animals stopped applying. So God advertised again, and this time, as well as asking for a good nightworker and dreamfighter, the ad said: *Pay in advance: one wish fulfilled*.

When Mutant heard of this, he thought: 'What if I ask him to make me busy. That's my only wish.' So he applied.

When God saw him, he was astonished. He couldn't remember making him. And when he heard the wish that Mutant wanted fulfilled, as advance pay, he laughed. Sleepy as he was, he actually laughed.

'Oh well,' he sighed. 'Granted. You'll certainly need to be busy to keep the nightmares off me. Yes, I grant you ten times the natural dose of busyness. That should be about right!' And he laughed again.

Mutant's eyes blinked furiously. Without waiting for God to say any more, he dashed outside. It was already dusk. What time did the Space Beings start their attack?

He raced over God's roof, through the forest and up a mountain. On the peak, he stood on his hind legs, waving his feelers.

Then he raced along the hills, from peak to peak. He raced the whole way round the circle of hills and back to God's house. He felt very strange. 'So this,' he thought, 'is what it is to be busy!'

He felt as if all his limbs were about to burst into flames. He had to move, and move very fast, and keep moving, to escape the feeling, which was actually rather awful.

But what now? Where were the attackers? It was dark. Where were the eyes he'd heard so much about?

He raced in a circle round God's house, up over the roof and back again.

And there they were – the eyes.

Mutant didn't wait for a second. He dashed straight in.

He felt the dizziness bounce off his hard skin. It knocked him off balance, but only for one of his lightning strides. Then he felt the dreadful suction pump clamped over his face. But he clashed his pincers and shredded it, before it could suck him inside out. Then the springy, hard, light bat hit him, but he clung to it, ran over the mesh, and down the handle, and over the fingers gripping the handle, and seized the wrist in his pincers.

A most horrible screech went up. God peered out through his window and saw an immense shape floundering in the darkness, and he heard trees crashing. Then a tearing cry of pain, and then more cries, and groans, going off, through the forest, with splintering tree boughs. The cries seemed to climb the mountainside, then go off up into space.

Mutant appeared in God's doorway. He was dragging something. At first God thought it was a Rhinoceros without a head. Then he saw it was a colossal hand. Mutant had brought him the nightmare's hand.

From that night, Mutant's life changed. He became God's bodyguard, and all the creatures heard about him with awe.

And he certainly did some amazing things. The Space Beings didn't stop trying to get at God. Every night Mutant raced through the forests and over the mountains, to and fro, to and fro, and here and there, over God's roof and around his house, all at top speed, and the Space Beings simply couldn't outwit him.

No matter what shape they took, he was ready, he was there, with his terrific activity.

One came as a fog, but Mutant grabbed a blazing log from God's kiln and raced through and through the fog till he found the heart of it – a kind of big soft spider dangling on a thread from space. When he plunged the torch deep into the spider, the whole fog fell as a two-minute rain of honey blobs.

Mutant licked his feet and tasted the honey blobs. He had seen the other creatures eating. In fact, they did little else but eat. This was the first time Mutant had tasted anything. He whistled with delight. He spent the rest of that night licking the leaves, the grass, even the bare ground.

'At last,' he thought, 'I've found something to live for.'

Next night, as he raced in his protective circles, he noticed a slender bamboo shoot growing beside God's door. 'Strange!' he thought, and raced on. By midnight, no Space Being had appeared, but the bamboo was as thick as an Elephant's leg, and its leaves leaned in through God's doorway. And then, as Mutant dashed over God's roof for the fiftieth time that night, he heard God groan on his bed.

Had the nightmare got through?

Mutant hurled himself at the bamboo, and crushed its thickness with his pincers. The splintering was also a screech, and all the leaves flew like knives. Mutant shook his head, like a Dog, and the bamboo toppled. Honey welled out of the mangled stump, and Mutant was still feeding there when God got up next morning. Looking at the stump and the fallen bamboo, God said: 'That reminds me. I dreamed. My spine was a bamboo tree. I was growing in a swamp. It was horrible. Then Man came in a canoe, cut me down, and made me into an organ pipe, a giant flute, and that was beautiful.'

Mutant, his pincers deep in the oozing honey, tried to smile.

Every night Mutant overpowered a different Space Being. But now he was not only defending God from Space Beings and the nightmares they came in, he was keeping up the honey supply for himself, since every Space Being, somehow or other, shed honey.

Feeding on the honey, his busy energy became

fiercer than ever. But something else was happening too. Mutant was growing.

At the end of the first month, after about thirty nights of victorious dreamfighting, Mutant was the size of a Camel. At the end of the second month, he was the size of an Elephant. 'God's bodyguard,' he cried, 'needs the weight.'

Now as he raced through the forest and over the mountains, he travelled along the deep lanes he had worn. His passing sounded like a motorboat, as his six feet pounded the earth.

God was sleeping well. He was so pleased with Mutant, he built him a special tower beside his own house. Mutant would race to the top of it, and survey space. During the day, to use up his busyness, he dug cellars under it, and deepened tunnels down to deeper cellars. He called the tower the Palace. And God, seeing him grow, changed his name from Mutant to Giant.

The other creatures began to be alarmed. For one thing, when was Giant going to stop growing? That worried them. He was already bigger than any of them.

For another thing, it was becoming quite difficult to sleep. All night long Giant was charging along his trails, through the forest, up the mountain, over the peaks, back through the forest, on his maze of different paths. And the din was terrific. It was like living in the middle of a permanent speedtrack. And not only was the noise impossible, the earthquaking was worse. He was getting to be so tremendously heavy. And every three minutes or so he let out a shattering roar: 'Make way for God's bodyguard!'

At last the creatures came to God and complained.

'As he gets heavier and bigger,' cried Sloth, 'he gets faster. He's forever shaking me off my branch, just by pounding past.'

'And the accident rate,' cried a Shrew, 'it's going up and up. Why can't he fly?'

Giant listened as he paused deep in the earth, working at one of his cellars. He dashed up and sprang out in front of the creatures.

'Complaints?' he bellowed. 'What do you want? Me or no me and God going crazy with nightmares? Which of you serves God as I do? Which of you will take my place to defend God?'

The creatures all sidled away. Giant certainly scared them. His eyes were really quite terrible, and he was obviously trembling with eagerness to attack some-body.

God frowned and scratched his chin through his beard. If it weren't for those Space Beings and the nightmares, he was thinking, the world might be a nicer place without Giant. He was getting to be a bit too much of a good thing. But so long as the Space Beings kept coming . . .

The night after that they stopped. Had Giant finished them off? He raced along his trails. On into the dawn, he was rushing from peak to peak, gazing into space, waving his feelers. Where were the Space Beings?

That was his first night without honey. But the second night was the same. And the third.

On the fourth day he lay still on his tower. He was thinking: 'What if Space Beings are over?' Then he whispered: 'What if the honey's finished?'

His legs jumped into action. He raced into the forest. At one point he stopped and roared: 'All creatures great and small will bring honey to Giant. Failure will be punished.'

He then seized Linnet by the scruff of the neck: 'Where is the honey? You pay your taxes in honey. And you pay them to me.'

Linnet squirmed. What could he say? So Giant flung him into one of the cellars under the Palace.

When Bullfinch, Newt and Giraffe had joined Linnet in Giant's cellars, the other creatures learned. They began to squeeze nectar out of the flowers, and brought it to Giant. Even Leopard brought him some on a leaf.

'Not enough,' roared Giant, and pushed Leopard down into one of the cellars.

Few of the animals brought much. Pretty soon the cellars of the Palace hummed like a great beehive with the sobbing and wailing of the imprisoned animals.

God realized something had to be done. 'Giant,' he thought, 'has gone crazy.'

When he asked Giant to let the animals go, Giant stared at him, incredulous.

'But,' he gasped, 'they didn't bring me any honey.'

God nodded, and keeping his voice very gentle and calm he asked: 'But does that really matter?'

Giant almost squeaked. 'Matter?' he cried. 'But if I don't have honey, how can I guard you? I need the strength.'

God nodded again. 'Very true,' he said. 'But,' he added, 'maybe I don't need guarding any more. The Space Beings have stopped.'

Giant let out a blasting screech, like a steam whistle, and stared at God thunderstruck.

'I serve you,' he bellowed finally. 'I am your body-guard. That is my life. Don't you understand what it means, to be the bodyguard of God?'

God gazed at Giant. 'This peculiar creature,' he was thinking, 'really has gone crazy!'

'Who else but I can fight the Space Beings?' Giant continued at the top of his voice. 'Without me you'd be a sleepless wreck, your Creation would fall to bits. So I need energy. I NEED HONEY!'

Giant stood there. He looked exactly like a house-size statue made of girders and ship's boilers, all glowing red-hot. His eyes looked like welder's flames. Even God felt quite alarmed. But then he had a brainwave.

'What about the Bees?' he asked.

Giant frowned and sparks crackled. 'Bees?'

'The Honeybees,' said God. 'Let all the animals go free, and Honeybee, henceforth, will work only for you.'

So Giant let all the animals go free, and waited. Now that his limbs were still his mind was going faster and faster. He was trying to calculate how many Bees he would need.

But God was also thinking hard, and at last he knew what to do.

First of all he hung a wet sack over the Sun. Next the Wild Goose and the Swan brought him snow. He modelled this snow into a figure exactly like Woman, but as big as himself. There she stood, in front of his workshop.

Now he sent Magpie to advertise a new job: a bodyguard for God's bride.

A bodyguard for God's bride!

All the creatures came running. Even Wild Goose and Swan gazed in wonder at the beautiful Snow Maiden. Was God getting married? The creatures were wild with excitement.

But Giant, too, had emerged. He stared at the dazzling white figure.

He was very angry. And when he spoke, he had difficulty forming the words, because all he wanted to do was roar with rage.

'All creatures,' he cried, 'will go home. The body-guard of God is also the bodyguard of the bride of God.'

God came out of his workshop. 'But, Giant,' he said, 'I thought you couldn't work without honey. The Bees will take some time, you know, getting you a good enough supply to start you off again. I'm afraid my bride needs a bodyguard now.'

'I don't need honey,' choked Giant. 'I am her body-guard. I am your bodyguard. I am the only bodyguard.'

'But she is so beautiful,' said God. 'Something will surely steal her. While you're racing about over the mountains, she'll be snatched by the Bridesnatcher from inside the Earth.'

'By who?' Giant had never heard of the Bride-snatcher inside the Earth.

God sighed. 'A terrible being. Worse than any Space Being. He comes light as a breath. Invisible as a breath. Soundless as a breath.'

'Test me,' cried Giant.

But God only shook his head.

'If she were to be stolen – ' he began. Then he stopped and sighed again.

'I'd find her,' Giant cried, 'I would never stop till I found her and rescued her.'

God seemed to think deeply. 'All right,' he said at last. 'But promise. If she is stolen, you will never stop till you have found her and brought her back.'

Giant nodded. He felt if he spoke he would burst into tears of rage. How could God doubt him?

'Swear,' said God sternly.

'I swear!' cried Giant, through his clenched teeth.

'Very good then,' said God. 'You are her bodyguard.' And as he went back into his workshop he casually drew the sack, now almost dry, off the sun.

The next hour was the most terrible time of Giant's life. The sun's great beams blazed down on the Snow Bride.

And as Giant stood, staring at her, she began to sink slowly into the ground.

He raced round her in tight circles, trying to see where she was going. But it was no use. And the moment came when the last glint of snow melted into the sodden ground.

He could not believe it. He stared at the place till the ground was dry.

Then he began to race to and fro over it, looking for a way in, and whimpering like a little puppy dog.

God came out. He stood there, simply nodding. He seemed to be beyond anger. And when Giant saw the grim look on his face he cried: 'I'll find her, I'll find her.'

'How?' asked God, and stood silent.

'Somehow, somehow,' cried Giant.

'However are you going to get into the crannies of the Earth, where the Bridesnatcher's carried her off? I knew this would happen.'

'Make me small, make me tiny,' wept Giant. 'I'll find her.'

'Well,' said God. 'If I did that, at least you'd have no problem finding enough honey. Very well, I'm relying on you.'

And God snapped his fingers.

Giant saw everything grow suddenly enormous. The grass blades towered far above him. The forest loomed like a green, stirring thunderstorm.

God looked down. Giant, no bigger than a fly, was scrambling over the crumbs of soil.

'Try every hole,' boomed God, high up in the sky.

'Try every cranny. And when you've found her, let me know.'

He went back into his workshop, whistling a little tune under his breath.

Then the Baboon danced up. 'Gee-up, Giant,' he laughed. 'She's getting further away all the time. Now you'll need your famous speed. Gee-up!'

And Parrot cried: 'Gee-up, Giant!'

And the Elephants, blinking sleepily, rumbled: 'Gee-up, Giant!'

Pretty soon, Geeup Giant was simply called Gee-upant.

'Gee-up, Geeupant,' laughed the Jackass.

Giant, now so tiny, began racing in and out of the wormholes. And he has never since been able to rest. Where can he ever find the maiden of melted snow? Where did she go? But still he races along, deep in forests, under all the roots, and far out over deserts, down every crack in the baking crust. He races over the world, unresting. Where could she be? Where is she?

'Poor old Ant!' sighs the Sloth.

Gozzie

To amuse his mother, God invented the little fluffy yellow Gosling, and gave it to her. She was very pleased. Its comical little eyes at the corners of its beak made her smile. And she loved its soft, broad, purplish webbed feet that waddled along with their toes turned in.

It followed her everywhere. At night it jumped on to her bed and slept as close to her as it could get. It was very proud to be the pet of God's mother. While the other birds watched from bushes and trees, or from high in the air, Gosling waddled along at her heels.

'Well,' he would say to himself, 'aren't I the lucky one!'

And the birds would mutter to each other: 'How did he do it? What's so special about him?'

Even as he grew bigger, and his yellow fluff became grey feathers, he still followed God's mother everywhere. And she still called to him constantly: 'Come on, Gozzie, have a nibble.' And she would feed him some delicious little bit of something from her fingers.

'He's lucky,' rattled Magpie. 'But wow! Isn't he ugly! And what a voice!'

It was true, Gozzie was ponderous-looking. He looked too fat, for one thing. And as he grew bigger, his fat belly sagged deeper between his legs.

But he didn't care. 'Jealous!' he'd quack. 'Absolutely everybody is jealous of me. Sometimes even I'm a little bit jealous of me!' And he laughed: 'Wak! Wak! Wak! Wak! Wak!'

'Ugh!' cried the Owls, covering their ears.

'You could be good for one thing,' chattered the Starlings. 'God's alarm clock. With a bit of practice at getting the time right.'

'Jealous!' quacked Gozzie.

But it was true. His voice was not pretty. His voice, in fact, was ugly. It worried him a lot. Sometimes, when he was sitting in the grass close to God's mother, perhaps when she was peeling mushrooms or shelling peas, he would think: 'How is it I'm so lucky in everything, yet have such a horrible voice?'

And sometimes he would listen to Thrush in the evening, or Robin, and he would feel so miserable he would actually weep. Then he would think: 'If only I could sing like that! I think I would exchange everything just to be able to sing. Yes, if I could sing, I don't think I'd mind living in the rough old forest. Or out on the windy river.'

Then he would go down to the river and swim a bit, dipping his head under the water so the other birds wouldn't see that he'd been weeping.

If only God had given him a proper voice!

Soon he was thinking about his voice all the time.

Worrying about his voice. 'I can't sing. I can only honk and yodel in a cranky way, and quack. I'd sooner be a fish.'

God's mother had no idea, of course, that her darling pet was so wretched. He never told her. He never breathed a word about it to anybody. He was too proud.

One day it was announced: the creatures were having another song contest. Everybody was wildly excited, as usual. All except Gozzie.

'Oh no!' cried Gozzie. 'I can't bear it. Oh! I think I'll go and stick my head in the mud of the river bed till it's over.'

The birds were sure the winner would be a bird. The animals, the reptiles and the insects had their champions. But they all secretly suspected the winner would be a bird.

Which bird? A favourite was Nightingale. A close runner-up favourite was Skylark. Another was Missel Thrush.

But suddenly – a sensation! Everybody was talking about Water Snake.

Water Snake was a new creature. God had never meant to give Water Snake an unusual voice. But something went wrong in her making. A lucky accident! Anyway, the result was, Water Snake had an absolutely stunning voice.

A delicious, liquid, heart-stopping voice! When she lifted her head up between lily pads, and sang a melody, even Alligator's tail curled slowly upwards, in an agony of pleasure. Yes, the beauty of Water Snake's voice was so keen it was painful.

When she draped herself on a floating log in some backwater, and sang a full song, practising for the competition, even God found himself rooted to the spot. Wild Bull set his brow to the ground and leaned on it, groaning softly. Flying Beetle lost control of his wings in his effort to listen. He fell into the grass and lay there, legs in the air, just letting the song happen to him. Other kinds of snakes, that were coiled in trees, became limp and simply slithered loosely to the ground, lying there maybe on their backs, motionless as long as the song lasted.

And Nightingale, Skylark and Missel Thrush, and the other favourites, fell silent.

It surely was an incredible song.

But nobody was listening so hard, or so painfully, as Gozzie. Yes, for Gozzie that song was pure cruelty.

'Oh!' he sobbed in the reeds. 'Oh! Oh! Oh! If only! If only! Why Water Snake? When God made me for his mother, couldn't he do me a favour? A voice isn't much of an extra. And I could have sung for her, his own mother.'

And he plunged his head into the mud beneath the water. But straightaway he lifted it out again, not to miss a note of the song.

Magpie decided to take action against the new rival of the birds. He flew out over Water Snake.

'Hey, knot-neck!' he bawled. 'When you stop sing-ing do you know what? You vanish into ugliness. Your ugliness is so impossible – you're invisible. We can't help hearing you, but do we have to look at you?'

Woodpecker joined in with a laugh: 'Hey, creepy, you've won a prize – for the wettest worm and the droopiest drape. Give us another spaghetti solo.'

Then Kookaburra came, with an even worse laugh. 'Nice of you to sing for my supper!' he cried and dived down, great beak wide open, to catch and gobble Water Snake. She dived under water in a flash, but only just made it.

After that, these three birds made Water Snake's life a misery. Whenever she lifted her head out of the water, to practise her singing, these three came flying, and Kookaburra made a grab at her.

'Seems like Water Snake's not in the running any more,' the birds said.

Meanwhile, Gozzie's heart was breaking. At last, he couldn't bear it any longer, and he told God's mother. She listened in surprise. She had never guessed.

'You poor darling!' she cried at last. 'Why didn't you say something before? Of course my son will make you into a singer. You just leave it to me.'

And gathering him up, big as he now was, she took him in to God. And she told God what was making her pet so unhappy. Gozzie simply laid his head over her shoulder and sobbed openly.

'Well, who'd have thought!' said God, and he

dropped into his chair. Gozzie's grief was so plain to see, God was quite upset.

'But what can I do now?' God asked helplessly. 'Once he's got his voice, he's got it for good.'

'You're God, aren't you?' cried his mother. 'Simply give him another voice. A standby. Any kind of decent singing voice. You're the Creator – think something up.'

'Well, I'll try, I'll try,' said God. And he leaned his brow on his hands. 'You'll have to give me time, though. It's not going to be easy.'

What on earth could he do? But then, as his mother went into the kitchen, crooning over Gozzie, God noticed a movement down in the corner of his doorway.

It was Water Snake. She had managed to reach God without being seen by the birds. And now she told him her tale. Her tears splashed on to the floor. God sat listening, deep in thought. What a day! First Gozzie, now Water Snake! It was all getting too much. At last he burst out:

'But what can I do? So the birds scream insults at you whenever you sing. And Kookaburra tries to grab you and gobble you up. Can't you stay silent under water? You're a water snake, remember.'

'And waste my beautiful voice?' cried Water Snake. 'Can't you get rid of those birds.'

'Certainly not!' said God sharply. 'Not once they're made.'

'Why don't you make me a bird?' wailed Water

Snake. 'Then they'd be on my side. It's all because I'm not a bird.'

When Water Snake said that, God slapped his brow. He had a sudden brainwave.

'Wait,' he cried. And he called his mother and asked her to bring in Gozzie. Gozzie, who was now a big, heavy goose, came waddling in, and stopped, craning his beak towards Water Snake. Water Snake curled up into a tight ball and peered out from between her coils. This looked like another bird to her.

'Now,' said God to Gozzie. 'Here is Water Snake.'

'I know, I know,' moaned Gozzie. 'The heavenly singer!'

'Well, how would you like to have her voice?' asked God.

'Me?' gasped Gozzie. And he jerked up his wings as if he might fall over.

He couldn't believe his ears. After all, this was God speaking. God did not make jokes.

'Wait, wait,' cried Water Snake. 'What's going on?' And she uncoiled and writhed herself into a tangle of question marks. Her brows came down and her black eyes scowled from under them. Her tongue flashed like a little whip.

'Will you be patient and listen,' said God. 'Both of you.'

Then he explained. He would remake them into a single creature. So Water Snake, inside Gozzie, would be a bird. And Gozzie, with Water Snake inside him, would be the singer of singers.

Gozzie blinked. The idea of having Water Snake's voice drove every other thought out of his head. That voice coming out of his mouth!

'Oh please!' he sobbed. 'Oh, that sounds wonderful! Oh, could it really happen?'

But Water Snake let out a screech and went lashing all over God's workshop like a firecracker.

'Never!' she screamed. 'Never! Live inside that stupid, ugly-looking goose? The birds say I'm ugly only because they're jealous of my voice and my beauty. I'm a beautiful black whip of water lightning. Oh I am, I am. And I love being me!'

'Listen!' cried God. 'Why don't you listen? Let me finish.'

Water Snake lay in a tangle, as God went on:

'I will make Gozzie the most beautiful of the birds. He will be perfectly beautiful. More beautiful than any other beauty. Beautiful without a flaw. And you will be gazing out through his eyes, seeing the whole world gazing amazed at you.'

'And singing through my mouth,' whispered Gozzie, 'seeing the whole world listening. Oh please, please.'

'The other birds,' said God, 'will no longer insult you. They will adore you. They will worship you. And with your voice, you will be – well – you know what you'll be. You will be the absolute star.'

Water Snake's tongue flickered.

'Maybe I'll – just try it,' she hissed. 'But if it doesn't work – '

'Try it!' said God loudly. 'Good. Close your eyes, both of you.'

Then he tossed Gozzie and Water Snake into his furnace of creative fire, brought them out magically white-hot, and with his magical hammer on his magical anvil pounded and beat the two shapes into one. The sparks flew. It all seemed to happen in a flash.

His mother brought a bucket of water up from the holy well and poured it over the finished creature with a crash and a great explosion of steam.

And there it stood, the new creature, in a puddle of water. Bigger than Gozzie, and white as fiery new snow. And there, peering out from under its brows, were Water Snake's black eyes. And Water Snake's black skin was there too, over the great webbed feet.

It turned its head on its snaky neck. God's mother saw how snaky her Gozzie had become. And when it looked at her she knew: this was no longer her Gozzie.

God planted his big mirror in front of this new creature. The head reared up, and out of the beak came a long hiss.

'Horrible!' It was Water Snake's voice, from the great white bird's throat. 'Let me out! Let me out!'

'But you're incredibly beautiful!' cried God. 'Look at you. You really do look like an Angel. You look like a bride in her lace.'

'I don't,' cried Water Snake. 'Look at my great fat body. I look like Gozzie, only bigger. Let me out!'

'Nonsense,' said God. 'You'll get used to it. Just stroll down to the water – but sing as you go. Then you'll see what the birds do. They'll fall out of the trees with surprise. And remember, you're gorgeous.'

Gozzie's great feet waddled out into the garden and down towards the river. As he went he stretched up his neck – and hissed.

Not a word came out. Not a note.

'Sing,' cried Gozzie to his voice. But all that came out was a funny sort of grunt. It wasn't even a honk or a quack any more.

God frowned, rubbing his chin. He watched Gozzie swim out on to the river.

'Give us a song now,' he called. 'It will sound wonderful over the water.' Gozzie stretched up his neck, but again all that came out was a hiss.

'What's wrong? Where's the voice?' shouted God.

'When you let me out,' cried Water Snake. 'Then I'll sing. Till then I sulk.'

'In that case,' shouted God, getting angry, 'you stay in there till you sing! Now sing!'

'Not till you've let me out,' screeched Water Snake.

'Sing,' ordered God. 'When I say sing, you sing.'

'Never never never never,' screeched Water Snake. 'Never till you let me out.'

God clamped his jaws tight shut and glared at the white shape on the river. Gozzie dipped his neck and upended his whole body, as if his eyes and beak were trying to bury themselves in the mud at the bottom.

'You've done it again,' said God's mother, shaking her head. 'Poor little Gozzie!'

'You're right,' said God. 'If ever I made a mistake, there's one.'

'It will need a new name,' said his mother.

'Hmmm!' said God. His mind was a blank. What on earth could he call such a mixture? 'Let's leave that to Man,' he said at last. 'I don't want to make another mistake. Man might get it right.'

How God Got His Golden Head

Poltergeist lived in God's workshop. Where had it come from? It had no idea.

It lived inside an old candlestick that God had carved long ago from a piece of driftwood. God never used the candlestick. Nowadays, if he worked after sunset, he worked by the light of his own eyes.

So the candlestick sat up on the shelf, collecting dust. And Poltergeist lived inside it.

Poltergeist had no shape, no weight, and not even God could see it.

'Am I a him?' it asked itself sometimes as it watched God bent at his work.

Or sometimes, when it saw God's old mother moving about in the shadows of her bedroom, it thought: 'Maybe I'm a her.'

It could fly. It loved to swoop about the workshop. It loved to fling things from one end of the room to the other. Most of all, it loved to hear things go smash.

Sometimes, when God's mother brought him a cup of tea, the cup would rise from the saucer, empty itself over God's head, then shatter itself against the ceiling.

Poltergeist would laugh silently and flit back into the candlestick.

Another time, when God went into his workshop one morning, he found the whole room upside down. There he was, walking across the ceiling, and looking up at the floor above him, with his chair, his work-bench, all upside down above him, and still on the workbench was his nearly completed Centipede. Was the Centipede having to cling, or was it just somehow lying there?

With a great effort, God twisted the whole workshop round, and got it the right way up again, with the floor under his feet. But now he saw something peculiar. In his mirror, everything was still upside down. How could that be?

He gripped the mirror in both hands and with a terrific effort he twisted everything in the mirror, to get it the right way up. And with a bang, he fell on to the ceiling.

Now everything inside the mirror was the right way up, but the workshop was upside down again.

On the shelf, the upside-down candlestick tittered.

Again, with an effort, God got the workshop the right way up. But once again, everything in the mirror was upside down. He turned the mirror's face to the wall and looked at the candlestick.

He knew there was something very funny going on in his workshop. And he knew there was something funny about that candlestick. Was there a connection?

Sometimes Poltergeist tried to take a hand in God's

work. As it watched him, working away, creating his wonderful creatures one after the other, it longed to do the same.

One day God made Wolf. Before he'd quite finished it, he sat back, pondering. Somehow, this animal was turning out too gloomy. It sat there on his bench, glowering at him. 'How can I brighten you up?' murmured God.

For answer, the Wolf yawned. But as it yawned, a blazing log from the fire soared across the room and disappeared down the Wolf's throat. The Wolf gave a yell and all its hair spiked on end. God managed to grab it, and hold it, while he reached inside and pulled out the log. But the Wolf was now on fire inside. Its eyes glowed and the froth boiled out of the corners of its mouth.

'What now?' cried God. 'Oh lord, this is a mess!'

'Something to drink!' cried Wolf. 'Quick, oh quick, a drink!'

God tried water. It was no good. He tried treacle. It was no good. He tried milk. No good. God tried all kinds of things, but he had to go to bed at last, leaving the Wolf chained to the leg of his bench, lying there in the dark with blazing eyes and lolling tongue.

When God came into the workshop next morning, Wolf was nowhere to be seen. The chain lay there, and the empty collar.

Then God noticed a few hairs sticking up out of the neck of his brandy bottle. He picked up the bottle and peered through the glass. There was his big Wolf, crammed into the brandy bottle. Its eyes seemed to squirm, pressed tight against the glass inside.

Carefully he broke the bottle. Wolf burst back to its full stretch and shot out through the open doorway with a yowl.

The candlestick chuckled.

This time God heard it. He grabbed the candlestick, strode to his doorway, and hurled the wicked object as far as he could. Instantly, with a crash, all the glass of the window behind him showered in over his bench and the candlestick rolled across the workshop floor.

'Tricks!' bellowed God. 'I'll settle your tricks!'

He snatched up the candlestick again, strode again to the doorway, and again, harder than ever, with all his strength, hurled it at the far sky. With a ringing crack it hit the back of his own head and bounced away over the workshop floor, as he fell on to his knees watching a shower of stars.

Carefully now, he put the candlestick back on its shelf.

Then he stood at his open door rubbing the back of his head and frowning, and listening to the Wolf, running through the deep forest, howling for whatever it might be that would quench the flame inside it.

Soon after this, one afternoon, God was dozing in his chair. Often in the middle of his work, he would doze off like this. Some of his best ideas came to him in these little naps.

He yawned, and felt a tickling inside his ear. Putting his little finger-end in his ear he felt a big round lump of ear-wax, simply sitting there, in the porch of his ear.

He half woke, looked at it, yawning, and idly flicked it away across his workshop.

By sheer fluke, it hit the candlestick, bounced to the floor, and rolled. Before it had come to a stop, God was asleep again.

But Poltergeist was awake. It peered out, and its gaze fastened on the ball of ear-wax. 'Did you knock?' it whispered.

It floated out of the candlestick, and sank to the floor. Close-up it gazed at the ear-wax. It poked the ear-wax. It picked up the ear-wax and gently rolled it between its palms.

Was this a little bit of God? Out of God's own ear? It was still warm with God's warmth. It was golden, like a kernel of sweet corn. And it was quite soft.

Poltergeist suddenly had a wild idea. It would make a creature out of this ear-wax. Poltergeist almost laughed out loud. It would make a creature not out of clay, like God, but one out of a little bit of God himself.

A creature made out of God! At the very idea, Poltergeist shuddered with excitement.

It had always wanted to make a bird, a swift, swooping sort of bird like a Swallow. It started to shape the ear-wax. Wings, and a tiny streamlined body, then the face.

But as it worked, it remembered God's Wolf. What if it made a tiny Wolf? Or better still a Dog. A Dog made of God!

This time Poltergeist did laugh out loud, and stared

at the thing in its fingers. But then in mid-laugh it stopped. The thought about the Wolf-Dog had got into the ear-wax. And there it was, with wings, like a bird, but with a little snarly face, and fangs, like a Wolfy Dog. And it was now very nearly black. That was all the dust from living so long in the old candlestick.

Poltergeist gazed at what it had made. Actually, it looked quite interesting. Different from anything else. But Poltergeist liked that.

The creature had no life, of course. But that didn't worry Poltergeist. Stealthily, it placed the tiny beast of ear-wax on the back of God's sleeping hand, and, with a plink! like a snapping harp-string, shot back into the candlestick.

When God woke he found himself looking at the tiny snarler on the back of his hand. At first he thought: 'I've dreamed another monster! This time a midget!' That sometimes did happen. Wart Hog had arrived like that. One night God had dreamed of a Wild Pig with a face like the root-ball of a torn-up tree, and it was trying to tip him out of bed. Next day he got the shock of his life when he walked in his garden and met Wart Hog itself, rooting up his tiger lilies and crunching the bulbs.

But now he saw that this new little creature had no life. So where had it come from? And what was it made of?

He had to admit, it was beautifully formed. 'Has my mother made it?' he wondered. Surely she would have given it life, because she too had the gift of giving life.

He blew the breath of life into its face. The creature

squeezed its eyes shut, then suddenly took off. It dithered about the room. It could fly all right, but it seemed to spend all its energy trying not to hit things. God smiled. 'Practise hard,' he said. 'Practice makes perfect.' Then he went back to work on Desert Rat.

The new-made creature beat its wings wildly. It had no idea what it was or where it was. It saw a wall spinning towards it, then a ceiling, then a floor. Every beat of its wings brought something rushing towards it. Or at least, that's how it seemed to the little beast, as it swerved and dodged and doubled back.

It kept seeing God, bent at his work. And suddenly, in mid-whirl, it had a brainwave: 'If only I could get into his ear! There I'd be safe!'

So it tried to attract his attention, flying to and fro in front of his face, between his nose and the Desert Rat, and crying: 'Let me live in your ear.'

But its voice was so thin God could not hear it. It was really a Poltergeist voice. The Poltergeist could hear it, and he smiled silently as he watched from his candlestick.

Then the Wolf-Swallow or whatever it was thought it might just as well fly straight into God's ear, whether he liked it or not. But at that very instant, God snatched it out of the air, and tied it to his harp by one of the broken strings.

'There,' he ordered. 'Rest a while. You're getting on my nerves.'

The harp leaned against the wall, at the back of God's workbench. For a moment the Wolf-Swallow hung head downward, peering up at the string tied round his ankle. 'What's happening now?' he thought. 'This life is all surprises.'

Then he tried to fly straight at God's ear. But the string round his ankle jerked him back, and he bounced fluttering against the other unbroken strings of the harp.

A shower of plinketty-twangling notes showered out of the harp, under the strokes of the wings.

The Wolf-Swallow couldn't believe his ears. He fluttered at the strings again, and another shower of notes sprinkled around the room.

He laughed. He suddenly felt joyful. Now he felt really alive. He forgot how dreadful it had been, reeling about in the air, with walls and furniture spinning towards him wherever he turned. He flittered again over the harp-strings, and back again, and to and fro, making the notes tumble.

God stopped his work and listened, astonished. He knew he had never heard music like this. And yet, somehow, it was familiar. It was a haunting, eerie music. Actually, it was partly Poltergeist music, but also partly music from God's own ear-drum. Nobody had ever played God's ear-drum, so God had never heard the music hidden in it. Inside the candlestick the Poltergeist clapped his hands, and hugged himself tightly and rocked to and fro with delight.

But much as he liked this music, God had soon had enough.

'Enough!' he commanded. 'Rest now. A little peace now.'

But the Wolf-Swallow would not stop. He had not had enough. He danced over the strings, flinging his wings, whirling on the end of his leash, hurtling to and fro across the harp like a mad hand, or like a mad glove rather, in a storm of notes.

'Joy!' he cried. 'Joy! Joy! Oh! Oh! Oh!'

He wanted to go on for ever. But God could not hear his cries of happiness. He caught him again, untied his leash, and was just about to toss him out through his open doorway into the world when he got a shock. When Wolf-Swallow saw that glare of daylight in the doorway, he knew more than ever where he wanted to be. He twisted from God's hand and like a black flash flew up and straight into God's ear.

'Aaaagh!' cried God, and clapped his hand to his ear. Then tenderly he wormed his finger-end into his ear as deeply as he could. Too late. The fluttering beast had gone right in. And as God wriggled his finger-end probing deeper, the creature fled in deeper. And now it was right inside God's head, skittering about among his thoughts. God clutched his head and strode about his workshop.

'Oh!' he cried, and 'Aaaagh!' and 'Eeeegh!' He turned his mirror to see himself. And there was his own bewildered face, upside down, with the upside down hands clutching his hair.

Then the creature dived down through his body into his heart. Suddenly, it felt at home. Everything here felt familiar and friendly. And here he found something even better than a harp. He started hurtling about inside God's heart, playing his heart-strings just as he had played the harp on the bench. But here the music was far deeper, stranger, richer.

'Wonderful!' he cried to himself, as he hurled himself about among the strings. And the more fiercely he played, the more excited he became.

But God felt all this as an awful sensation. It was more than he could stand. He couldn't hear any music. All he knew was the ghostly plucking and twangling, the fluttering wings of the Wolf-Swallow right inside his heart, as if his heart itself were flying about on wings inside his ribs.

He beat his chest with his fists, trying to drive the crazy creature out through his mouth. But it wouldn't come out. And it wouldn't stop. He roared, like his own Gorilla, pounding his chest. His mother came running in. She stood there helplessly, wringing her hands, watching her mighty son hurl himself about the workshop, beating his chest, and roaring as if he hoped to blow his own heart right out through his mouth.

God looked at his mother with terrible eyes. 'What shall I do?' he wailed. 'What's the cure? Don't you know the cure for this?'

She only went on wringing her hands, and all the wrinkles around her eyes began to shine with tears.

'Ask the Earth,' she said at last. 'The Earth's the wise one.'

God almost fell out of his workshop. He stumbled on to his hands and knees and crawled over his lawn. He beat on the lawn with his fist.

'What's the cure for this?' he roared. 'Tell me the cure
for this!' Then he kneeled up, and grappled at his chest
with his great hands. It was as if he had a fire in there,
like the Wolf. Only this wasn't a flame. This was a
living and fluttering shadow, with a bird's wings and a
Wolfy head, whirling inside his heart.

The Earth suddenly spoke. For a second God
managed to hold still and he heard:

'Ask the Moon.'

God ran to the top of the nearest hill where, as it
happened, the full Moon was just rising.

'Moon!' he shouted. 'What is the cure for this! This –
whatever it is?'

His mother could see him outlined against the full
Moon, like a mad dancer. And she heard the Moon's
whispering reply:

'Ask the Sun.'

God uttered a roar of anguish and disappointment.
But he set off, bounding over the ridges of forest and
the ravines. And the Wolf-Swallow played more wildly
than ever. He couldn't tell what God was doing, but it
seemed to him that God was dancing, leaping up and
down, with now and again a somersault. So the Wolf-
Swallow played louder, harder. He uttered thin howls
of ecstatic joy. It seemed to him, the more wildly he
hurled himself into his music, the more wonderfully he
broke into huge new gulfs of music, grander and more
vast. 'More!' he howled to God. 'More! More!', urging
him to leap higher, to dance more madly. But God only
cried: 'Oh! This is horrible!' as he stumbled across the

world to where the Sun was sinking behind the sea.

'What's the cure,' he bellowed, 'the cure – for this?'

And he beat his chest as his bellowing shout ended in a roar, that seemed to shake the flat, resounding shine of the sea.

The Sun was silent awhile. Then the voice came, out of the centre of the fiery ball.

'The cure,' said the voice, 'is severe.'

'Anything!' shouted God. 'I don't care! Anything!'

And again his shout ended in a bellowing roar and he pounded his chest.

'The cure,' said the Sun, 'is to put your head into my furnace.'

'What?' squeaked God. He couldn't believe what he'd heard. Also, his voice was wearing out.

At that moment the crazy player inside his heart flung himself into new efforts. He knew God had become still. He thought he'd simply stopped dancing. So now he tried to get him going again, dancing again, with new rhythms. He strummed and slammed, he plucked and leaped.

God placed his hands in the sea and leaned forwards towards the Sun. With all his courage, closing his eyes, and wrapping his hair and beard around his face, he thrust his head deep into the white-hot furnace of the Sun.

For a few moments, he thought he'd made a shocking mistake. Surely, he thought, I am going to burst into flames. I'm going to explode, like a barrel of petrol.

He could feel all his atoms glowing towards flashpoint.

But then he realized his heart was quiet.

From inside his heart, the Wolf-Swallow was gazing into the glare of God's head. He did not like this at all. And as the glare became more intense, and the Sun's great heat began to brighten through God's body, he became afraid. He felt his wings growing soft. They no longer plucked at the heart-strings.

A sudden terrible fear came over him. As the dazzling glare surged down through God's neck and shoulders, he suddenly knew he was going to melt. He had to move fast.

God felt a peculiar sensation behind his knee. It moved down into his ankle. It writhed across the sole of his foot, under the skin.

With a puff of smoke, the winged and wolfy-headed creature of ear-wax shot out from under the nail of his left big toe.

It whirled down to the Earth, a black falling star, and plunged through a crevice into a deep cave. It hung itself under the ceiling, in a dark niche, panting.

God pulled his head out of the Sun. He had been bright before, but now he glowed, as if his head itself had turned into Sun. All his hair and beard dazzled whitely, and vibrated, like the element in an electric lamp, like white-hot white gold, and his face glowed like pure, new, polished gold.

He came back to Earth and stood on the hill behind his workshop, listening. From far away, among all the evening hubbub of Earth's creatures, he could hear a new sound. A tiny thudding. He smiled. It was the heart of the mad musician, the Wolf-Swallow, hanging upside down in the damp dark of its cave, squeezing its eyes shut against the terrible memory of the Sun.

This was Bat. Now he comes out only after the sunset. He hurls himself about, plucking at invisible strings. He is remembering God's harp and the music that poured out of it under his wild flying. And he is remembering God's heart, and the fantastic music he'd played inside there, that had made God himself roar and leap.

The Moon and Loopy Downtail

The Poltergeist in God's candlestick could not rest. He'd watched and watched, as God fashioned the perfect creatures. And they really were perfect. Even the most horrifying ones, like Angler Fish, Lamprey, Giant Medusa Jellyfish – no matter how ghastly, they were still somehow wonderfully perfect. They made Poltergeist want to weep and laugh and writhe, all at the same time, they were so perfect.

If only he could make something like that! Something so perfect. Finally, he knew he would have to have another go. His efforts so far had all gone wrong, in one way or another. What he needed to do, he felt, was to let his fingers imitate God's fingers exactly. He needed to follow him exactly, in every move he made, as he created a creature. But how could Poltergeist do that, without God seeing him? And if God were ever to see him – well, there was simply no telling what he would do. Probably cram him into a blazing star and hurl him into outer space.

Also, he needed something more. It wasn't good enough just to imitate. 'Inspiration! That's what I need,' cried Poltergeist. But where could he get that?

Where could a Poltergeist find inspiration?

One night he was thinking of this after God had gone to bed. As he pondered, a white light slowly filled the workshop. It was the full moon, rising and looking in through the window. Poltergeist saw the great white disc reflected in God's mirror. He stared at that reflection. How brilliant and pure it was! Somehow it looked better in the mirror than it did in the sky. But then, as he stared at that great light in the mirror, it seemed to Poltergeist that he heard something. A voice.

'Do it,' said the voice.

'Do it?' thought Poltergeist. 'Do what? And whose voice is this, anyway?'

'Do it,' said the voice again. And suddenly a dazzling idea came into Poltergeist's head. He stared at the Moon's reflection. He suddenly saw how he could make a creature that would be exactly like God's. What a brainwave! He was so excited, his candlestick wobbled on its shelf. But he forced himself to wait. Yes, he would do it. The very next chance, he would do it.

'Thank you very much, Mystery Voice,' he said to the Moon's reflection.

Seeming to smile, the Moon rose slowly past the top edge of the mirror and the workshop became dark.

That next day, Man came to God asking for a friend.

'But I've already given you Woman,' said God in surprise. 'Delightful Woman. And you've also got Baby. I thought you were happy.'

'Oh, no complaints,' said Man. 'It's just that when

53

I'm away in the forests sometimes, I don't know how it is, I get an eerie feeling.'

'Eerie?' queried God.

'I know,' Man went on, 'the world is a wonderful place. A wonderful wonderful place. I wouldn't have it one bit different. But it's also – well – a bit spooky. At times.'

'Spooky?' murmured God, fingering his beard. 'Hm! I wonder what you mean.'

'You know,' said Man, 'I'd like somebody along with me, a happy little friend, so I could say: "Come on, let's be off!" or "Did you hear that?" or maybe: "Why don't you go and have a look behind that bush?" '

'Hm!' said God. 'I see. A trusty companion.'

'Whatever you think would do the job,' said Man.

God thought for a moment, then said: 'I'll tell you what. You have a go. Come on, make just the friend you want, and I'll breathe life into it.'

'But I can't make things!' cried Man.

'Oh yes you can,' said God. 'You've never tried. But I'll show you. Just do as I say.' And he hoisted a big ball of fresh clay on to his workbench.

'Now first,' said God, 'do this.'

And so he began to show Man how easy it was to shape an animal. All you did was imagine it, then fill up the shape of the thought with clay.

Man suddenly had a vivid picture in his head of the friend he wanted. He laughed with excitement as God guided his hands.

Poltergeist watched closely as Man's fingers, guided

by God, worked the clay. He felt intensely jealous. If God could teach Man, why couldn't he teach Poltergeist? Still, in its way this was a perfect lesson. Man was learning. And as Man learned, Poltergeist, too, tried to learn.

Poltergeist could soon see this was going to be a very pretty creature indeed. Lovely slender legs, a lovely bright face with a long, very sweet snout, and brown eyes, really startling brown eyes, almost golden eyes. And a grand tail sweeping upwards, bushy.

God showed Man how to take particular care with the teeth, the toenails, and getting the angle of the ears just right. They worked on it through the whole day. Evening came, and at last the creature seemed to be all but finished. God stroked it, making its fur glisten. Then God set it on the floor and turned it this way and that. He was thinking: 'Because of Man I've put far more care into this than into anything else for quite a while. I want it to be absolutely perfect. And I think that's it. I really think there's no more to be done, except for the life.'

Now Poltergeist knew his moment had come. He had to move fast. Once God breathed life into this creature, it would be too late. God would send it off with Man, and Poltergeist might never see it again. He might never get another chance to do what he planned to do.

So he hurled himself into action.

With a terrific scream, like a thousand Elephants, he tore a wide circle through the forest around God's home.

'Fire!' he screamed. 'Fire! Fire!'

God looked up. The leaping flames reflected in his eyes. So sudden! He hadn't even smelled the smoke. He dashed out where the Poltergeist's scream was being taken up by the real Elephants, along with the screams of the Leopards, the Monkeys, the Cockatoos. All the creatures of the forest were yelling at the top of their voices: 'Help! Help! Fire!'

God set to work, beating out the fire with the palms of his broad hands, occasionally clapping his hands in the clouds to bring out the down-pouring rains. And the rains did come down. Even so it was touch and go as he coughed and choked, reeling in the clouds of sparks and rolling smoke, while the trees exploded around him like soft bombs, and Man bounded home through the forest to warn his wife, and get their belongings together, ready to flee to safety if the fire began to blow that way.

All this time, Man's finished but still unliving companion stood in the middle of the workshop floor, like a stuffed animal, gazing at nothing with bright golden eyes, waiting for life.

Poltergeist sat up on the windowsill, peering at the shaking red mane of the great fire. Now and again, when it looked as though God might be getting the upper hand, Poltergeist shot out and with another tremendous scream blazed a new roaring and popping and cracking and crashing swathe of flames into some untouched part of the jungle.

So God laboured, fighting the conflagration till past

midnight. Finally he stamped out the last spark. The rain stopped and the sky cleared. The last reddish billowings of smoke blew off the full Moon, which now hung over the scorched forest tremendously bright and round. It was so bright, it threw God's shadow blackly ahead of him as he trudged home.

Aching, he flopped into his bath. Wearily he crawled into bed. It was only then, as his head sank into the pillow, that he remembered the bright ready creature on his workshop floor, waiting for its breath of life. He smiled. 'Tomorrow's a new day,' he murmured, and was already asleep.

Just as Poltergeist had planned!

The workshop was dark, except for the shaft of brilliant moonlight that came in through the window. Poltergeist did not want to light candles. God might see the glow in the crack of space at the bottom of his bedroom door. Poltergeist had a better idea for lighting up what he wanted to do. Pausing only to listen for God's steady breathing, he lifted the big mirror off the wall, and propped it leaning, nearly upright, against the nose of the new, wonderful, but still lifeless creature, which now stared with unseeing eyes at its double in the mirror. It looked as if it were sniffing at the nose of its own image in the mirror. But the strangest thing was, Poltergeist had so positioned the mirror that the full Moon shone behind the creature's image, reflected in the glass. Its black pricking ears were silhouetted against the Moon. It looked to be wearing a bright silver halo, a dazzling halo.

With the help of the bright moonlight, Poltergeist began to work fast. He pulled out a good-sized lump of clay from beneath God's workbench, and simply filled in that reflected shape in the mirror. This had been his great brainwave, and it worked. All he had to do was pack the clay into that perfect reflection, like clay into a mould. It sounds complicated, but for a Poltergeist it was the easiest thing. Because it was so easy he could work very fast. The Moon rose swiftly from behind the creature's ears, but it still had not passed out of the top of the mirror when Poltergeist had finished. He gave his creation one last close inspection, checking every hair, then he lifted away the mirror from between the creature that Man had made with God's help and the creature he himself had made by the light of the Moon. And there the two creatures stood, facing each other, nose to nose, exactly alike, drenched in moonlight.

It was then that Poltergeist saw his only mistake.

Because he'd leaned the mirror against the nose-end of the creature made by God and Man, the two creatures were not merely nose to nose – they were actually joined at the nose.

Poltergeist examined the noses. There was no sign of a join. One nose simply grew into the other. There was no doubt about it, he'd made a funny sort of mistake here. He stared and stared at the single nose of the double creature. What could he do? Time was passing. Dawn would be here soon, and God would probably choose this day to get up early. What could be done? But he was still thinking when the bedroom door swung open and God strolled into the workshop yawning and stretching.

With a click, Poltergeist was back in his candlestick. And God gazed down, bemused at first, then puzzled, then baffled, then outraged, at the eight-legged monster, the strange double creature that stared at itself with four eyes.

'What?' he shouted, incredulous. His first thought was that he must have sleepwalked. 'Somehow,' he thought, 'I came out here and I did this in my sleep. How else could it have happened?'

He couldn't think of any other explanation. He laughed then, and scratched his head. 'Maybe,' he thought, 'maybe I did just that. What a peculiar business!'

Suddenly he was filled with curiosity. What if he gave this oddity life? How would it manage?

Still not properly awake, he kneeled down and looked under the joined noses. The chins were separate but just touching, just kissing. He pulled them gently down, and with a single breath blew life into both the open mouths at the same time.

But even as he sat back he knew he'd made an error. The four eyes of the double creature rolled wildly. They stared at each other in dismay, over the joined noses, then stared sideways at God. And the eyes seemed to be saying: 'What's this? This can't be right. What's happened?'

Their upcurling bushy tails waved uneasily and they whined softly.

At that very moment, Man appeared in the doorway.

'Just in time,' said God. 'I've just finished your new friend.'

Man stared, licked his lips, blinked, and stared again. Maybe God would explain it to him. 'Are you sure it's right?' he said at last.

'What do you mean, am I sure?' cried God. 'Did you ever see such a pretty beast. Such pretty legs. And ears. And eyes. Such a gorgeous fur. Look at its ruff. And what a tail! One of the finest ever tails.'

'Two of them,' corrected Man.

God frowned. 'Try it,' he said sternly. 'Give it a chance.'

Man looked carefully at the joined noses, and now the two beasts rolled their eyes sideways looking at him. They couldn't bend their heads because their noses had no joint. It was just as if the nose bone went from between the eyes of one to between the eyes of the other.

'Take it,' urged God. 'You might be surprised.'

But the creature could not move. If one had walked forwards, the other would have had to walk backwards. And how many creatures do you see walking backwards? So this creature stood, and swivelled its eyes towards God, then towards Man, then back to God, and whined again.

'Pick it up,' said God. 'Show it you love it.'

And so Man picked up the double beast, one in the crook of each arm, with the joined noses over his head, and carried it home.

Woman gave a short, sharp laugh when he set it down in front of her. Then she stared at it.

'Is it a piece of furniture?' she asked.

Man simply sighed, and went on gazing at the eight-legged freak.

'I know!' cried Woman suddenly, laying her finger in the middle of the long connecting nose. 'Chop it through here. Then we'll have two for one. One for you and one for me. Get the axe.'

The four eyes jerked wildly this way and that way, between Man and Woman, then stared at the finger. First the nose! Now the axe!

Man carried the creature back to God and explained Woman's idea.

'It's a risky thing,' said God, 'to interfere with creation. I'll do it. But we might be sorry. It might cause trouble.'

'Oh!' said Man. 'What's a bit more trouble?'

So, with his thumbnail, God nipped through the middle of the long nose that the two creatures shared. With a yelp, they leaped apart, shaking their heads and pawing at their snouts. God caught one of them, examined the raw nose end, then spat on it and rubbed it.

The other whined and its tail drooped.

'Come on, then,' said God. 'You too. Don't sulk.'

He did the same with that one. And the two creatures, exactly alike, stood there, quite separate, licking their noses. One of them gazed brightly at God, and wagged its upturned tail. The other gazed sidelong at

its partner. Its tail still drooped. It yawned, then licked
its chops, blinked and gazed out through the doorway.

'Now, my dears,' said God, 'that might have felt a bit
painful. But I had to do it, because I wanted to give you
both very special noses. Very very special noses. Now
you both have the keenest, keenest sense of smell. You
might well ask: Why do we need this special sense of
smell? Well, why do you need it? Do you know?'

God looked at them as if he expected them to answer.
Uptail gazed at him boldly, his big ears angled forward,
his eyes gold and bright. Uptail did not know. Downtail gazed at him with lowered head. His eyes were
grey, not gold like Uptail's. And his eye-pupils were
tiny pinpoints of black. His ears moved, angling this
way and that. He did not know either. He gazed at
God, waiting for an answer. But as he waited, his ears
never stopped listening to all the sounds of the world.

'Your special sense of smell,' said God, 'is to lead you
to your maker. Nothing will really satisfy your nose
except one thing: the smell of your maker. Once a day,
you will have to lick the fingers of your maker. Now,
away with you.'

Man was happy. 'Come on, boys,' he cried.

God called after him. 'Just remember. You don't have
two creatures there. You have two halves of what was
created as one. Halves can be very odd. Keep your eyes
open.'

Man strode off, one creature leaping around him,
jumping up to him, putting its forepaws on his chest,
the other following a few paces behind, its nose and its

tail low to the ground, occasionally lifting its head and staring at flowers, as if it heard sounds coming out of them.

From the first moment, the two were quite different. There was no doubt which one was going to be Man's companion. Uptail never left him. When he sat, it rested its chin on his knee and gazed up at him. When he walked, it walked just behind him, keeping its nose within inches of his knee. When he spoke to it, it laughed silently and dangled its tongue.

Man was delighted. 'Fido, I'll call you,' he said. 'Hey, Fido!'

And Fido yelped with excitement, seeming to bounce, then stood with its forepaws on Man's shoulders and gave his whole face a wash with two swipes of its big wet tongue.

'Come on,' cried Man. 'Let's be off!' And he strode away into the forest, with Fido bouncing beside him like a thing made of springs.

Woman looked at Fido's partner. 'I suppose this one's mine,' she was thinking. As she looked into its eyes, it lowered its head, lowered its ears, and glanced away. For some reason she suddenly felt slightly afraid. The house seemed very silent. 'I'll have to make friends,' she thought.

'Come on, Loopy,' she called in a sudden loud voice, and slapped her knee. To her horror Loopy, as she'd called him, leapt up, its legs rigid, all its hair spikily on end, its ears flattened, and snarled into her face. Such a horrible, long, deep snarl that its whole body vibrated.

'Now, now!' she chided. 'Don't you like your new name? Isn't Loopy quite a good name?' And she reached her hand towards him. She knew she must not let him see she was afraid. She made her voice cheerful and soft. 'Come on, give me a lick, like Fido.'

But it made no difference. Loopy flattened to the floor, his whole face bunched up like a cloth being wrung out, and again he gave a crashing snarl.

Then, with one leap, he was out through the door and gone.

Woman ran to the door and bolted it. She sat down and looked at her hands, which were trembling. 'Well,' she whispered, 'he didn't give me much chance to make friends with him!'

When Man came home and heard her story he remembered God's words about the two halves. Meanwhile Fido searched all over the house, busily sniffing at everything. Man thought: 'Is he glad the other's gone? Or does he miss him?'

Fido seemed to have read his thoughts. His tail swung in great circles, he squirmed his body and reared up at Man with whining yelps. He licked his face again, then licked his hands and fingers. Then across to Woman and before she could stop him he did the same to her, whimpering with happiness. He seemed to have his forelegs almost around her neck.

'Strange!' thought Man. 'Very strange!'

Fido certainly seemed happy.

*

But out in the forest, Loopy was not happy at all. He wandered along, sometimes his nose to the ground, sometimes sniffing the wind. 'I'm looking for something,' he was thinking, 'but what is it?'

Tirelessly he went on. After a while he began to trot. Then he began to run. As he ran, a thousand smells came drifting past his keen nose.

'But which is my maker?' he thought. 'God said my nose would lead me to my maker.'

He ran on and on through the forest, then out on the ridges of the hills. Sometimes he stopped and sniffed and licked at a stone. Then he ran on. Night fell and he was still running.

Later that night, as Man's fire glowed red, and the potful of mushroom soup bubbled on the flames, Uptail Fido sat with his head on Man's knee, gazing up at the sparks of red fireglow reflected in his eyes. When Man spoke, Fido laughed silently. And when Man fondled his head, Fido tried to tie his fingers in the slippery loose knot of his tongue.

But suddenly they heard a strange sound. A new sound. Man, Woman and Fido looked up. The round, full, bright Moon now sailed directly above, a great white blaze in mid-heaven. The new sound seemed to come from the Moon. Or perhaps it echoed off the Moon.

High on a rocky hill, above the forest, sat Loopy Downtail. His nose, glistening with God's spittle, pointed at the Moon. Out of his mouth came the new sound, the strange, wailing howl. The forest was motionless. No other creature made a sound. Were they all listening to this new noise among them? What was Loopy Downtail trying to say? Was he crying or singing?

He seemed to be trying to talk. Man and Woman could almost hear words and sentences in the ups and downs of that thin, faraway howl. He seemed to be winding his voice round and round the moonlight. It made Man think of the long tongue of his new companion, Fido, licking and winding round his fingers.

But Fido did not like it at all. He growled a deep angry growl. He did not like to see Man and Woman listening to that howl. He knew who was making it. He wanted to rush off into the forest and silence it. He wanted to chase Loopy Downtail away, right out of hearing.

'Shhh, Fido!' said Man. 'Quiet, boy.'

Woman had stood up. She had turned away from the fire, facing the forest.

'Eat your soup,' said Man. 'It will go cold.'

But she went on standing there. 'Listen to it,' she whispered. 'Only listen.'

And there she stood, ignoring Man and his new friend, and her soup, simply listening to the long wavering howl that seemed to be climbing and climbing towards the Moon.

The Gambler

God was making Frog. He had almost finished. There it sat, green and yellow, with its front toes turned in, and its great golden eyes gazing from two bumps on top of its head.

No fur, no feathers, no scales. Just shiny smooth skin, like wet plastic.

God stared at the creature thoughtfully. It looked very bare.

'Maybe some feathers,' he murmured. 'Or short velvety fur, like Mole. Hm! That might be nice.'

But before he could give anything else to Frog, a shadow fell across the open doorway of his workshop. Man stood there, his face glowing with excitement.

'Well, well, well!' said God. 'What a nice surprise! Any news from the great forest?'

Man held out his two clenched fists in front of him, their backs upwards. He stared at God brightly.

'Guess which holds the black pebble,' he said.

God smiled. Did Man truly think he did not know? He saw the black pebble glowing darkly through the knuckles of Man's left fist. And in his right fist, veiled with a faint pink, he could see a white pebble.

'So what's this?' asked God.

'Don't you see?' cried Man. 'It's a game. Woman invented it. She said: "If you choose which fist holds the black pebble, I'll give you a kiss. But if you choose the white pebble, I give you a slap." '

'So what did you get?' asked God.

'Three slaps. I got it wrong three times in a row.'

'A lot of fun, eh?' smiled God.

'Pretty exciting,' said Man. 'The fourth time I got a kiss.'

God laughed. 'Well,' he said. 'And what if I get it wrong? What do I get? A slap?'

Now it was Man's turn to laugh. Or at least, his mouth laughed. His eyes stayed excited, bright and wild.

'Well,' he said, 'you could give me power to create an animal. A living animal. How about that?'

God became more interested. What sort of animal would Man create, he wondered, if he had the power to do it? He would love to test him. Would he create a beautiful thing? Or a gigantic monster? Or what?

'Very well,' God said. 'Let's say the black pebble is in that hand.' And he tapped the hand that he knew held the white pebble. With a strange croaking shout of glee, Man opened the fist and showed God the white pebble in it.

'Wrong!' he yelled. 'Give me the power.'

God pretended to look surprised. 'Oh dear!' he said. 'What a good thing I'm not going to get a slap. Yes, you've won the power. Use it wisely. Only one creature, remember. What a clever game!'

Man leaped from the workshop doorway on to the lawn. He stabbed both fists into the air. 'I have the power to create,' he yelled. 'I won it!' And he bounded into the forest, eager to tell Woman that he had defeated God in her great new game, and that now he had the power to create a new creature.

God smiled and turned to the Frog. He was still thinking so hard about Woman's strange invention that he forgot all about the extra trimmings he was going to give to Frog. He simply breathed life into it as it was, all bare-skinned and cold-looking.

As Frog drew his first breath, and looked out through his golden eyes for the first time, he croaked: 'Which fist holds the black pebble?' and held his clenched fists up to God. God sat back and laughed. Somehow he had breathed the idea of Woman's game into Frog.

'But you haven't got a pebble,' he said. 'You can't play this game without pebbles.'

'Where are my pebbles?' cried Frog, staring at his empty palms. 'Give me my pebbles, so I can play.'

'You'll have to look in the river,' said God. 'That's where the pebbles are. All colours.'

'Where's the river?' cried Frog. 'Quick! Quick! I can't wait!'

God took him to the river. Frog plunged in and in no time came up with a black pebble in one hand and a glittering jewel in the other. He held out his fists.

'Guess the black,' he croaked.

'And what if I get it wrong?' asked God.

69

'We change places,' cried Frog. 'I become God and you become a Frog.'

'And what if I get it right?' asked God.

'I give you a kiss,' said Frog.

God laughed again and tapped the little green fist in which he could see the black pebble glowing through quite clearly, just as clearly as he could see the jewel glittering through the other one.

Frog stared at the black pebble on his open palm. God had won. He shrugged. 'Oh well!' he sighed. 'It was a try.' And he jumped back into the river.

'Hey!' called God. 'What about my kiss? Come on – pay your debt. That's the law. If you win, you collect your winnings. If you lose, you pay. That's God's law.'

Frog surfaced and blew him a kiss.

God went laughing back into his workshop. But Frog stared after him. A breeze rippled the river, and Frog felt suddenly very cold. Why did he feel so cold? He dived to the river bed, and buried himself in soft silt, trying to find warmth.

Frog soon realized that every creature had more than him. They all had either fur, or feathers, or scales. Or teeth. Or horns. Or tails. He had only his thin smooth skin. And no tail.

Or they had beautiful voices. Or loud alarming voices. Roars, bellowings, whinings. Or clear, lovely song. Frog could only croak, with a funny little gasping croak.

Also, the other creatures were nearly all wonderful

movers. They could fly. Or they could run. They could hurtle about in the bushes and the treetops, or over the stony ground. They could build nests among the spines, or dash through the thorns.

Frog couldn't do any of these things. He had not a single one of these useful ways. He could only crawl very slowly. He could swim, sure enough. But not like the fish, that flashed through the water like bright thoughts, and spun on a twinkle, or vanished into pure speed. All he could do was swim from the bottom of the water up to the surface. And from the surface back down to the bottom. But that didn't seem like very much.

'God forgot to give me the extras,' he muttered to himself. 'I don't have a single thing except what I look like. The other creatures have everything. It's God's fault that I'm so cold and have nothing.'

But then he thought about his black pebble and his jewel. Yes, he had those. And they were something. And suddenly, down there in the silt, he burped a tremendous bubble. It wobbled to the surface and burst there with a booming croak. Frog had just had a most fantastic brainwave. Quickly, he started to search among the river gravels. He had no difficulty in finding another black pebble. Another jewel took a bit more finding, but pretty soon he had one, exactly like the first. Now he had two of each. He put them in the pouch under his chin.

Crocodile was lying on a sandbank, imitating sleep, when suddenly Frog popped his eyes above the surface of the water quite close to the great creature's nose.

'Wakey, wakey!' cried Frog. 'I've got a new game.'

Crocodile's first thought was: 'What a plump little snack!' But he pretended to be interested. 'Oh really?' he said. 'What sort of game?' As he spoke, he moved his feet slightly, ready for a quick rush and a clashing snap.

Frog held out his fists. 'One of my hands holds a black pebble. The other holds a jewel. Which holds the jewel?'

'And what happens if I guess correctly?' asked Crocodile, shifting his chin slightly.

'Well,' said Frog, 'you can eat me.'

'And what if I get it wrong? Obviously you can't eat me,' said Crocodile.

'In that case,' said Frog, 'let's see. Eating me is pretty serious. So it has to be something to match. I'll tell you what. If you get it wrong, you give me all your fangs.'

Crocodile smiled. 'Stupid little beast,' he was thinking. 'Right or wrong, you're my starters.' But he said: 'OK. It's a deal. The black pebble is in your right hand.'

Frog opened his right hand, and there lay a jewel. 'Your fangs are mine,' he croaked. 'And you have to pay up. It's God's law.'

To his absolute horror, Crocodile felt something like a zip fastener unzipping down either side of his jaws, top and bottom, and saw his teeth tumbling out on to the sand. Quick as lightning Frog gathered them all up and stuffed them into his mouth. Crocodile saw them bulging in the baggy pouch under Frog's chin.

Frog couldn't speak, his pouch and mouth were so crammed with Crocodile's fangs. They stuck out between his tightly closed lips at all angles. He gave Crocodile a big wave and dived out of sight. Crocodile let out a toothless roar of fury and flailed the sandbank with his immense, jagged tail – whumpetty-whack! But what could he do? He had lost the game and his teeth were gone. He was astonished. He simply lay there and wept.

Very soon after this, the great black-maned Lion was drinking at the river's edge. He had just eaten an entire Wart Hog. Very salty. But he drank warily, because he knew the river hid Crocodile, with his sudden rush and his dreadful fangs. So Lion jumped back a yard when two golden eyes popped up a yard from his nose. He stared at the green, flat-mouthed face of Frog.

'Who are you?' he growled.

'I am Frog,' croaked Frog. 'And this river is my gambling casino. Do you want to play? Have you the courage to gamble?'

'Play?' rumbled Lion. 'Gamble? For what?'

Frog held out his fists.

'One of my fists holds a black pebble,' he croaked. 'And one holds a jewel. Guess which holds the jewel?'

'Why should I guess?' growled Lion. But then Frog began juggling the black pebble and the jewel from hand to hand, very fast. Lion couldn't help staring at the flashing jewel.

'Well,' said Frog. 'If you guess right, you get the

jewel. You can keep it under your tongue, so when you roar your mouth will flash with beauty and all the animals, and the Lionesses as well, will come closer to look.'

Lion blinked.

Frog held his hands behind his back and wriggled his shoulders. Then suddenly brought his fists forward.

'Which?' he cried.

'But what if I guess wrong?' purred Lion.

'Oh, in that case,' said Frog, 'let's see. How much is this jewel worth? Quite a lot. I'll tell you what. If you guess wrong, you give me your roar and your mane.'

Lion laughed with surprise. He was thinking: 'If I lose, I'll whack my great spread hooky paw down on that silly little head, and I'll simply take the jewel off him.'

'OK?' cried Frog. 'Is it a deal?'

'It's a deal,' said Lion. 'And the jewel is in your left hand.'

Frog opened his left hand and there lay the black pebble. 'You've lost,' he croaked. 'And both your roar and your mane are mine. And the loser must pay without fail. It's God's law.'

Then to his horror and bewilderment, Lion felt his mane tearing off like a great Velcro collar. He tried to roar with rage, but to his worse horror no sound came from his throat – only a dry whistle.

And there stood Frog, in the shallows of the river, packing the mane into a tight bale. 'Better luck next time,' he roared, and Lion flattened back his ears in the blast of sound from Frog's mouth – a blast of genuine Lion roar, out of that tiny mouth!

Then Frog was gone, down to the bottom of the river. Lion staggered to the top of a nearby ridge and lay down. He was stunned. How had it happened so quickly? No mane. And no roar. He covered his head with his great paws, and let the tears seep down through the furry wrinkles of his great face. His chest was heaving with rage. But what could he do? He had lost.

So Frog started his amazing career as a gambler. He challenged every animal. 'If you win,' he would say, 'you can eat me.' Or: 'If you win, you get this big jewel.' No animal could resist.

The forfeit for losing was always the thing they valued most: their fur, or their speed, or their strength, or their tails, or their beautiful feathers. Elephant lost his trunk and his tusks and his great ears. Giraffe lost her superb tail and her thrilling jigsaw spots. Tiger lost his stripes, his leap, and the talons of his right front paw. Humming Bird lost her brilliant cloak of feathers and had to hop about like a tiny plucked chicken the size of a beetle. Cobra lost her fangs and Rattlesnake his rattle. Rhinoceros lost his horn, his sense of smell and the toughness of his thorn-munching mouth. Weasel lost her dance and the whiteness of her belly. Porcupine lost his spines and Skunk her stink weapon and her gorgeous feathery black tail. Jaguar lost his black rosettes and the power of his green gaze. Macaw lost his fiery feathers and the beak that could crack a brazil nut.

And so on. Every animal lost their best possession to the cold-eyed smiling Frog. Frog stored all these winnings in a cave under the river bank. And never once did he lose. Oh no, he was far too smart for that. How could he lose?

What the animals did not know was that Frog was cheating. That had been his brainwave: how to cheat. That was why he had collected two black pebbles, and two jewels.

When he said: 'Which hand holds the black pebble?' both black pebbles were in his pouch, while his two fists each held a jewel. The guesser could not possibly win. Whichever hand he then chose for the black pebble always held a jewel. And when Frog said: 'Which hand holds the beautiful jewel I just showed you?' he had already hidden both jewels in the pouch under his chin and each of his fists held a black pebble. He was so nimble and swift with his hands, no animal ever saw him do the trick. And none of them ever suspected a trick. It was the first time any of them had ever gambled. They were all still so trusting!

But what was Frog going to do with his winnings? His plan was simple. When he had won enough, he was going to go to God and gamble again with God – this time using his trick. Yes, he would cheat God. And the deal would be, when God lost he would have to let Frog use and wear all his winnings as his very own, whenever he wanted. So he would be able to stroll out in his Porcupine armour. Or he would leap across the plains like a Gazelle. Or he could shake down a treeload of ripe fruit with his Elephant trunk. And he would always be warm, wrapped in his Otter's pelt with its seal-fur lining.

But what about the animals who had lost? They were raging, weeping, wailing, whining. At first they had been ashamed of losing their most precious possessions, and had kept their losses secret. But soon they were telling each other. Frog had defeated them all. Frog was worse than a tyrant. He was taking everything from everybody with his two little green fists and his great wide green smile and his cold golden eyes.

The animals came to God. They told him about Frog's game. 'You've made him too lucky,' they cried. 'He never never never never never loses. He's taken everything we had.'

God listened gravely and nodded. Frog had certainly been busy. Finally he said to them: 'Go home quietly and leave it to me.'

As God sat on his veranda, thinking what to do about Frog, he saw a movement on his lawn. Frog was crawling slowly towards him. God waited as Frog heaved himself slowly up the steps and on to God's veranda, where he squatted, pulsing his chin pouch and gazing up at God through his brilliant eyes.

'What's the news today?' asked God in a friendly voice. 'How are you enjoying the river?'

Frog's answer was to hold up his two fists. 'The

game!' he croaked. 'Remember? Let's have another round. I challenge you.'

God waited a moment, then said: 'I'll tell you what. First, we play your game, then we play mine. How about that?'

Frog lowered his fists. He wasn't sure he liked the sound of this.

'What's your game?' he asked.

'Oh, you'll see,' said God. 'Quite exciting, in its way. Let's play yours first, then I'll show you mine.'

Frog showed God the jewel and the black pebble. Then he held his hands behind his back and fumbled there. Finally, he brought his two fists forward.

He had a special gambling voice. 'Which hand holds the black pebble?' he cried.

'And if I win?' asked God.

'Whatever you like. I'll give you a kiss if you like,' said Frog. And he laughed a croaky laugh.

'And if I lose?' asked God.

'Then you let me wear and use all my winnings as if they were my own,' cried Frog. And his chin pouch pulsed. He knew this was the big moment. Also, he knew God could not win, because both black pebbles were already in his mouth. His two fists held only the two jewels.

God pondered and gazed at the little fists, pretending to think deeply. He could see quite clearly that neither fist held a black pebble. He could see both black pebbles lying together in Frog's chin pouch, like eggs in a nest.

At last he said: 'I think I have it.'

Frog waited. His raised fists trembled slightly. What if God should see through his trick?

But God reached out his forefinger and touched Frog's left fist. 'That one,' he said. 'There's the black pebble.'

Frog opened his hand slowly and showed God the jewel. 'I'm afraid, God,' he said solemnly, 'you've lost.'

God sighed and slapped his knees. 'Your luck,' he said, 'is unbeatable. It's unbeatable.'

'And are all my winnings now truly mine?' cried Frog eagerly. 'That was the deal.'

'Yes, that was the deal,' said God. 'They're yours as if I'd given them to you when I made you. What a pity though. This will be terrible news for the rest of the animals.'

'They'll get used to it,' cried Frog. 'When I had nothing at all I nearly got used to it.' And he turned to go. He had scrambled and flopped down a step or two when God said:

'Wait a minute. Now you have to play my game.'

Frog stared.

'Come on,' said God. 'That was the deal. You can't possibly lose, you know that. You never lose.'

Frog wasn't so sure. He had never played anybody else's game. He heaved himself back up on to the veranda. He suddenly felt quite chilly.

God was holding out both his open hands, palm upwards. On his right palm sat a tiny ball of clay. Frog looked at the clay. 'Is that your black pebble?' he asked in a low voice. God chuckled.

'Yes,' he said. 'In a way. Actually, I was thinking I'd give this to Man, to make his new creature. You remember how he won the game against me? He won the power to make a creature. I thought this might help him.' And he chuckled again.

What was God up to? Frog felt very uneasy. He licked his lips with his long tongue. 'OK,' he said. 'Let's get it over. What do I win if I win?'

'Well,' said God. 'What would you like?'

Frog thought for a moment, and licked his lips again. 'If I win,' he said, 'you have to give me perfect luck. So that I never never never lose a game. No matter what. Ever ever.'

God raised his eyebrows. 'Very well. That will certainly be a huge prize. Why, you could gamble for the whole creation and everything in it.'

'And win it,' said Frog with a broad smile.

'OK,' said God. 'It's a deal. Now, which hand holds the clay?' And he simply turned his hands over, closing them as he did so.

Frog was secretly overjoyed. 'God doesn't know how to play the game,' he thought. 'He's forgotten to hide his hands behind his back while he juggles the clay about between them.' But he pretended to think hard.

'By the way,' said Frog. 'You've forgotten to say what I have to pay if I lose.' Frog was smiling to himself. He was so sure of winning. God really did seem not very clever.

'Oh goodness! How stupid I am!' cried God. 'Well, yes, now let's think. Well – I'll tell you what. Everything you've won off all the animals – if you lose you give it to me. That's not much to set against the whole creation, is it? I can't think of anything else.'

Frog frowned. For some reason he felt confused. His head was whirling. He stared at God's fists. At least, he knew which held the clay. So he didn't really have to bother about losing. How could he lose?

'It's a deal!' he croaked. 'And the clay is in your left hand.'

God turned his left fist over and slowly opened it. Frog stared at the empty palm. Empty? Empty? How could it be empty? 'Where's the clay?' he wailed. And his body seemed to freeze to a block of ice. Had he lost? Had he lost everything? All his winnings? No! No!

God shook his head gently. 'I'm afraid,' he said, 'you've lost. You've lost everything you ever won.' Opening his right hand, God showed Frog the ball of clay.

Frog's eyes had gone dry. He blinked them and licked them to wet them.

'Everything?' he whispered. And he drooped. He seemed to sink into a little heap, till his chin rested on the floor between his toes. His eyes were closed.

'I can't bear it,' he whispered. 'The animals will eat me alive.' He crouched there silent. But suddenly he moved.

'Give me another chance!' he cried. 'One chance. Oh, please, God. One little chance. One more round.'

'Very well,' said God. 'But it will have to be my game.'

Frog nodded weakly. 'Anything you say, God. But give me a chance.'

'OK,' said God, 'this time the ball of clay gives you power to change yourself, in a flash, to whatever you want to be. So if you choose the clay, that's what you win.'

Frog stared greedily at the little ball of clay. His hopes perked up a little.

'And this,' said God, 'is a hop.' And opening his left hand he showed him a tiny rose thorn.

'A hop?' asked Frog. 'What's a hop?'

'You know,' said God. 'Hop, hop, hop. Hippety hop. Pretty useful in a tight corner. So even if you don't get the clay, and the power to be anything you want – '

'I get the hop,' whispered Frog.

God nodded.

'Now choose,' he said. And he held out his two fists. Once again, he hadn't bothered to juggle the ball of clay and the rose thorn. Frog stared at the right fist – the one that had held the clay. But he wasn't going to be caught again this time.

'The clay is in the left,' he croaked.

God opened his left hand and showed him the rose thorn.

At that moment, a Lion's roar shook the air. Elephant was trumpeting through his trunk. Humming Bird whizzed among the jacaranda flowers. The plains and the forests shook with joy as all the animals found their losses suddenly restored.

Quickly, without another word, Frog hopped back towards the river.

And God sat smiling, watching him go, and listening to the joyful uproar of his creation. He tossed the two rose thorns on to the table, and carefully took the tiny ball of clay out of his ear.

'You can't beat God,' he chuckled.

The Screw

God looked up in dismay. What had happened to the Sun? The light was failing.

There, in the middle of the sky, the Sun darkened. It wasn't an eclipse or a cloud or a dust storm. Yet the Sun was glowing a weird red. Slowly, as God watched, it turned purple. Then dark indigo. Then the Earth went dark.

All around him, with a roar, the cries of the creatures went up. Panicky screeches of birds caught in the dark far from their roosts. Wailing and hooting of the great herds of Antelopes, only halfway through their eating. Shrieking of the mice, dashing blindly into the wrong holes. Yelling of the Owls in delight at the early start.

God climbed up the sky and began to inspect the dark Sun. It was still very hot. His breath sent rainbow colours writhing over it as he turned it on its axle and peered for faults. No good. He would have to open it up and examine the works.

Chimpanzee, who had swung up behind him, clinging to the string of his apron, reached out to touch the huge gloomy globe.

'Watch it!' cried God, and slapped Chimp's hand

away. 'Touch that with your fingernail,' he warned, 'and it will frazzle you to the armpit. It's not as cool as it looks. The black heat is fiercer than the white. What are you doing here anyway? Get back to Earth.'

Then gently he began to unscrew one of the Sun's hidden screws.

Dangling from the apron string, Chimpanzee watched. And now God looked round for somewhere to put the screw. Everywhere was sky. Finally, he nested the screw carefully on the buckle of his sandal, and started on the next one. Soon he had four screws snuggling there, in the buckle of his sandal, while he began to ease open the trap door in the belly of the Sun.

At that moment, Chimpanzee reached out and with the tip of his finger and thumb took a screw.

His screech startled God so badly, he almost let go of the massive panel of the trap door, which would have banged down on his head. He only just saved it. He glared round in fury.

'Ape!' he roared. But he ignored Chimpanzee's flailing hand with its scorched finger and thumb. He was watching that screw falling through space. At the same time, he could not move to do anything about it. He held up the heavy trap-door panel of the Sun with one hand, while he reached cautiously down to rescue the three screws from his sandal buckle with the other, and put them between his lips. Then with his freed hand he cuffed Chimpanzee and sent him spinning down after the falling screw. Chimpanzee had not let go of the apron string. When the blow came, he clutched it even tighter. So he fell, still clinging to the apron, which had been torn off God's waist, and now fluttered above the falling Chimp like a half-open parachute.

'Find that screw!' God bellowed through his closed lips. 'When I've done this job I shall need it.'

When it reached Earth, the screw fell through branches and buried itself in dead leaves at the foot of a tree. Chimpanzee, falling the same way, crashed through the branches and bounced on the dead leaves. He lay there a moment, stunned. Then sniffed. A new smell!

He sniffed at his scorched hand in the darkness. Not quite that. Then he saw a glowing spiral of smoke rising from the dead leaves beside him. He parted the leaves and saw the screw, in a nest of smouldering leaves. Chimp was not brilliant, but he had his little flashes. And straightaway he knew what had happened. He knew what this was.

A baby Sun!

Poor old God was so dumb! Now Chimp knew why the Sun had gone dark. God simply hadn't understood. How could he know about babies?

Chimp was wildly excited. But as he peered into the glow, something came blundering out of the under-growth behind him. Chimp was shouldered aside, and who stood there but Wild Boar, gazing joyfully into the pulsing den of little flames, where the screw was beginning to glow again.

'Come on! All of you!' squealed Wild Boar. 'A bit of

the Sun's fallen off. We've got it to ourselves!'

Chimp could hear the whole family of Wild Boar storming through the forest. He had to move fast if he was going to save the Sun's child. These pigs had no idea. They would probably trample it out, or lie on it with their thick skins. He shook God's apron in front of Wild Boar's nose.

'This,' he announced in a loud voice, 'is God's apron. As you can see. And God said: "Wrap up the baby Sun, which you will find hidden in the dead leaves, and bring it to me." And he said: "Here, wrap it in my apron." '

Wild Boar stepped back and blinked. What was all this about God? Wild Boar was afraid of God.

Quickly, Chimpanzee folded the glowing screw and the smouldering mass of dead leaves into God's apron, wrapped it all up and, crying 'God is waiting', he set off at a run.

Fast as he ran, the rumour ran faster. The wild pigs were blabbermouths all right. Panting along, he heard Toucan shriek: 'Chimp's got a bit of the Sun! He's stolen it!' Then he heard Bongo bray: 'Chimp's stolen the Sun's heart!' Then he heard Anaconda howl: 'Chimp's pinched the Sun! No wonder it's dark. Chimp's got the Sun! Chimp's killed the Sun!'

And on all sides the creatures took it up: 'Chimp's pinched the daylight!' and 'Chimp's robbed God!' and 'Chimp's got the Sun in a bag!' and 'The Sun fell and Chimpanzee's eaten it!'

'Here he is,' screeched Fruit Bat. 'He's running away with the Sun. Catch him.'

And so, with Fruit Bat screeching above him, the running Chimp could hear all the creatures stumbling after him through the forest. 'Save the Sun!' they were screaming, and 'Chimp's got the Sun. Catch him!'

'Oh!' he cried. 'Foolish beasts! Brainless boobies!'

And still hugging his bundle he leapt into the cave of the chimpanzees.

'Who's that?' yelped his wife, from her cosy ledge.

Chimp didn't answer. Instead, he unrolled the apron. The glow of the screw in the smouldering leaves reflected from all the gems embedded in the cave walls and ceiling, and in the eyes of his wife.

'It's a bit of the Sun,' she cried.

'No,' he shouted. 'Don't you see? It's the Sun's baby. I saw it born. Look! I knew you'd love it.'

He had to shout. The din of all the creatures outside the cave was terrific, and growing louder. There were more every minute. And the floor of the cave shook with their commotion.

'What's going on out there?' his wife shouted. But Chimp couldn't hear her for the uproar, and he didn't see her lips move in the glow of the screw, because at that moment Buffalo bounded into the cave.

All the creatures outside fell silent.

'Where is the Sun you've stolen?' thundered Buffalo. 'You're under arrest.'

Chimp moved his mouth, but no words came out. The very sight of Buffalo, with his great eyes glowing red in the screwlight, and his black body glistening, had knocked all the words out of him.

But his wife had her brainwaves too. It came to her in a flash.

'Oh Buffalo,' she cried, 'thank goodness you've come. Quick, before it dies. Look, you can see it's dying. It's the newborn Sun. Oh! Oh! We have to save it. We have to keep it alive.'

And she pointed to the dim glow of the screw, in its leaves. Buffalo stared at the screw. Depending on how you thought, it could look to be growing slightly brighter, or fading slightly duller. It was very hard to be sure.

'Quick!' cried Chimp's wife. 'Bring in all the animals. I need them all. I know how to save its life. But I need their help.'

Buffalo was confused. But maybe she was right. If the Sun had shrivelled to that crumb of glow, it surely was in a poor way. It did make him think of a new-born calf, trembling there and not quite sure if it could ever get up. Yes, it certainly looked as if it needed help. It needed a nudge of some kind.

'Quick!' yelled Mrs Chimp, and she slapped his buttock. Then she turned and whispered to her husband.

Buffalo brought all the creatures crowding in.

'Keep to the walls,' he bellowed. 'Give it lots of air. It's only just born.'

Buffalo made a good policeman. Red eyes bobbed obediently round the walls of the cave, under the sparkly gleam of the gemstones.

Chimp had gone out, but now came in again with

God's apron stuffed with dry dead leaves. He was doing exactly as his wife had told him to do. Then he came in again with twigs and sticks. Then again with lumps of broken dead branch. He made a gigantic heap of all these, while the creatures surrounded the glow in a circle of red eyes.

His wife was now explaining to all these creatures just what had to be done.

'This,' she said, 'is the newborn Sun. But, as you can see, he's very feeble. He needs strength. He needs help. He needs encouragement.'

The eyes glowed. Chimp was arranging more dead leaves over the screw and blowing on it softly. The whole lot suddenly flared. Little flames jumped and tossed up a few sparks.

'You see,' she cried. 'Even just looking at it you're giving it strength. But what it really needs is to feel at home.'

The eyes blinked, flickered and glowed again. There must have been fifty different animals in there, and over two hundred birds, with quite a few reptiles.

'What we need,' she went on, 'is to make this place like Heaven, where the Sun lives. Now you – ' And she pointed to Hare. 'You be the Moon. Come on.'

Hare tottered forward, uncertain. What did it mean, being Moon? 'How do I be Moon?' she muttered.

But Mrs Chimp was pointing at Anaconda. 'And you,' she said, 'you are the Planet Mercury.'

'The Planet Mercury?' boomed the great snake. 'Has it legs?'

'And you,' she pointed to Leopard. 'Be Venus.'

Leopard blinked, and twirled her tail tip.

So Mrs Chimp went on. And in no time she had them all ready. Wild Boar was the Planet Mars. Lion was Jupiter. Buffalo was Saturn. Horse was Neptune. Hyena was Uranus. Rat was Pluto. And Wolf was the One Without a Name.

All the rest she spaced around the walls in twelve groups. Each group had three or four animals, but mostly they were birds, no two the same, and all of them more and more excited.

'You,' she said to them all, 'are the Constellations. The fixed stars. You all stay where you are. But get ready to sing. When I start singing, all you – sing your heads off. Sing as if you were blazing stars.'

Then she turned to the nine chosen animals. 'And you,' she said, 'are the Planets. You can sing too, but mainly you have to dance. Now, Moon?'

Hare pricked up both ears, then flopped them again. She was wishing she had never come.

'Start dancing around the Sun,' ordered Mrs Chimp, 'just as the Moon in the real Heaven dances around the Sun in the real Heaven. Go on. Start. Close to the baby.'

Hare lifted her very big feet and hobbled a bit, feeling foolish.

'Dance,' yelled Mrs Chimp. And Hare leapt. Then, getting the hang of it, leaping and flinging her limbs, she capered around the bright fiery screw, where Chimp crouched feeding more dead leaves and now a few twigs into the merry little blaze.

'Now me,' sang Mrs Chimp. 'I'm Earth!'

And to the absolute amazement of all the beasts there, she began to twirl and leap around Hare, and Hare twirled around her, and they both twirled around the struggling little fire which the black hands fed with more and more sticks.

'Now, Mercury!' yelled Mrs Chimp. And Anaconda, keen to show off his magnificent curves, came writhing over the cave floor, and spun and knotted and unknotted the most stunning dance, around the blazing screw, outside the twirling Moon and Earth.

'Come on, Venus,' yelled Mrs Chimp.

Leopard leapt into the dance as if she'd practised for months. She seemed to be twisting through her own signature over and over in giant, ferocious flashing letters, with a whizzing flourish of tail. And she couldn't help it: as she spun and writhed and somersaulted around the others, she began to sing. It was if her wild contortions were squeezing the song out of her, like a mad and bounding concertina.

'Now, Mars,' yelled Mrs Chimp.

Wild Boar seemed to explode into dancing. He whirled like a top. He cartwheeled like a Catherine wheel, his tusks glittering in the throbbing flames of the screw, as Chimp fed in more leaves and bigger sticks. Sparks swarmed up, and the song coming out of Wild Boar resounded like a great iron bridge played by girders for drumsticks.

Soon, the whole lot were whirling there. On the outside, close to the Constellations, Wolf, a shaggy, raggy shape, danced on his hind legs with fiery eyes, his head flung back, letting a weird, wailing twist of song come straight up out of him, biting it off in lengths with savage clashings of his long jaws. Closer to the fire, Rat was going round and round, bouncing like a ball, singing in a deep, surprising bass voice, and each time he bounced was like the boom of a deep drum. And round and round, closer to the fire, Horse bucked and cavorted, like a rodeo jumper, all electrical flashings and shudderings, and seeming to shower off sparks, at the same time singing in a thrilling counter-tenor voice. Then next, closer to the fire, Buffalo. That was something. The dance of the Buffalo! And the song! Then Lion, who seemed to whirl in tatters of fiery air, like a dancer of seven burning veils. Then Wild Boar. Then Leopard. Then Anaconda. And on the inside, close to the blaze, Hare and Mrs Chimp, round and round and round.

And the Constellations, their eyes brighter than ever as the blaze grew and flung up its long orange tongues, they couldn't keep out of it. They began to jig where they stood. And all the birds sang as if every bird wanted to deafen the rest.

After a while, Chimp simply heaped all his branches and logs on to the fire, which now poured straight up like an upside-down waterfall of flame roaring into a cloud of smoky sparks. Then he sat back amazed, listening to that incredible noise, and watching the wild, whirling shapes of the animal Heaven, and the huger, wilder whirling shapes of their shadows on the glittering walls.

How long did it go on?

The animals didn't care. They no longer knew where they were, while their limbs flew and their song shook the mountain over the cave.

They never heard Chimp's shout. And they never noticed, as he dodged through the dancers, and stood in the cave mouth, waving his arms and shouting.

But then his wife did notice. She stopped dancing. Hare banged into her and went sprawling into the ashes of the fire, which were soft and warm. The fire was out! How long had the fire been out?

That broke the spell. The singing faltered. The dancers staggered to a panting stop. Then in silence they all stared at the cave mouth where Chimp's black shape was silhouetted against the bright sunlight.

Of course, they all rushed out under the recovered Sun.

'Success!' they sang. 'We got the Sun going!'

God was coming through the forest. He stopped, watching the creatures scattering joyfully. Chimp, standing in the mouth of the cave, saw God, and suddenly he felt horribly guilty. He'd forgotten something. What was it he'd forgotten?

'My screw,' said God. 'Have you got it?'

But that was the first Disco.

Camel

Camel was a mistake. He was simply made wrong. He stood in God's backyard, where the different kinds of clay and the fuel for the kilns lay in heaps, and he knew he was wrong.

And he felt wrong all over.

He opened his mouth, which was a bit like a horse's mouth, but longer, droopier, and somehow wrong. He opened it and strained. A groan came out. Then he strained again.

God could see that Camel was trying to speak.

Camel wanted to cry: 'Why have you made me like this? I'm all wrong. Take me back and remake me.' But nothing came out.

God did try to remake Camel. But it was no good. When the inside's wrong, the outside can never be right. He tried different tails. All seemed wrong on Camel.

He tried different feet. In the end he put back the first set – great, spreading, foolish feet that they were.

Camel's hump seemed badly wrong. But when God took it off, Camel fell on his nose. So he had to put that back too.

Finally God gave up, and Camel stood there with his head like a giant sheep, his neck like an old snake looking out of a tree, his back like a sand dune, and his long knock-kneed legs like a photographer's broken tripod.

He stretched out his neck and groaned. He wanted his groan to say: 'Remake me.'

But God shook his head. 'My first real failure!' he sighed. 'I'll have to scrap you, I'm afraid.'

Camel flung up his head. 'Scrap me?' He knew what that meant. It meant going on to the spare-parts heap.

He swung round and got his legs going. He went out through the yard gate in a cloud of dust. No matter how wrong and horrible he was, he didn't want to become nothing but spare parts for other creatures.

He loped into the middle of a valley full of dry thorn bushes, and stood there, hoping nobody could see him.

God would have chased Camel, but at that moment Man walked into his yard with a bleeding head. Woman was supporting him.

'The hair's not enough!' she wailed. 'It's no protection at all.'

'What's happened?' cried God. He was horrified to see that one of his best inventions had been damaged.

Man was so busy holding his head, and Woman was so busy comforting him, and God was so busy looking at the great scratches on Man's forehead, that none of them saw a dark shape leap up into the tree beside the gate. The boughs shook for a moment, then two green eyes peered out through the shadows of the leaves.

'Did you fall?' cried God.

'It was Monkeys,' Man gasped. 'A Monkey tried to claw all my hair off.'

God saw what was needed. He had just prepared the skin for a new kind of Pig. It hung on the line. Now he took it down, and with a few skilful twists – there it was. A hat. A new protective hat. Almost a helmet.

He spat on Man's wounds, which healed instantly, and fitted on the helmet.

'Oh!' cried Woman. 'But it's so cute! Oh, please, God, me too. A Monkey could get me too. Oh, please, a hat for me too.'

'Quite easy,' murmured God. This time he took the skin of a big bushy sort of Weasel he'd been thinking about. The skin of a Fisher. With a few deft folds and tucks, there it was – finished. A pretty fur hat, with the tail dangling behind. Woman gave a squeal of pleasure as she fitted it on.

'Now you, God,' she cried. 'One for yourself. Let's all have hats.'

The green eyes in the dark tree jerked upwards a little, getting a better view, and blinked rapidly. Then they glowed, fiercer than before, watching the hats.

God smiled. These hats were a brilliant new idea. Man looked more powerful. Woman looked prettier. He scratched his beard and thought: 'Well, what about it? Why not a hat for me too?'

Suddenly, at that moment, he felt uneasy. He could feel something watching him. He turned. But he saw nothing, because the green eyes in the dark tree had closed tightly, just in time. They knew they glowed.

'This creature that attacked you,' said God. 'Are you sure it was a Monkey?'

'He thinks it was,' said Woman. 'But let me tell you, God, that was no Monkey. Monkeys don't have hooked claws. They have fingernails like me. Monkeys aren't bald.'

'Bald?' cried God. 'You say it was bald?'

The green eyes in the dark tree opened again and stared.

'Take no notice of her,' said Man. 'It was pitch black in the jungle.'

But God was frowning. 'Did you see footprints?' he asked.

'Like a Frog!' cried Woman. 'A Frog the size of a Gorilla.'

The green eyes blinked and became slits.

Man tried to change the subject. 'What about a hat for you, God,' he said. 'How about it? How about the whole sky? That would be some hat!'

'With the shooting stars!' cried Woman. 'And birds flying in it. And a thundercloud for a crest. And rain falling!'

Both God and Man laughed at that.

'A heavenly hat!' cried Woman.

That night when God went to sleep, he wasn't thinking about a hat. He was thinking about those footprints like a giant Frog's.

'So the Demon is back on Earth,' he whispered. 'And it sounds as though he's after Man.'

As he lay thinking in the dark, a small Bat came creeping down the wall, head downwards. It moved slowly. Its green eyes were tightly closed. Finally, it was hanging just above God's head.

It was the Demon! Sitting in the tree by the gate, it had heard and seen everything about the hats. And now, after making itself into this tiny Bat, it hung near God's head, trying to hear God's thoughts.

It was true, this Demon had grabbed at Man's head. But all he'd wanted was the hair. Actually, what he had really wanted was Woman's hair. But in the gloom of the forest he had grabbed at the wrong head. His wife had sent him to steal Woman's hair. And she wanted this thick mass of ringlets because she herself was as bald as the Demon himself.

The Demon didn't dare to go back to her without something. She was a terror. He was frightened of her. Sometimes, he thought he might just run away, and never go back to her at all. But he didn't even dare to run away. He always went creeping back, usually carrying whatever she wanted.

She always wanted something. She was so jealous of God's Creation that she wanted to make another exactly like it, but inside the Earth, under the Red Mountains. She sent the Demon out to steal God's creatures and plants. She now had a great many down there, though they had a poor time of it in the dark. But she was never satisfied. She always wanted more. And at the moment, her craze was to have the long thick hair of Woman.

But now the Demon had an idea. Instead of Woman's hair, he would get God's hat. He had seen how wonderful Man and Woman looked in their hats. And the hat hid the hair. Just as it would hide the baldness. Therefore a hat was better than hair. He could just hear himself saying to his wife: 'Here you are, my beauty, here is God's hat for you. I snatched it from God's own head for your sake.'

Then she would let out a shriek of delight that would probably shatter a big jug. 'God's own hat!' she would hiss. 'On my wicked little head!' Then she would laugh and give him a kiss that would tear half his moustaches out by the roots.

So the Demon listened deeply to God's thoughts. And after about an hour he could tell that God was no longer worrying about Demons. He had begun to think about hats. He was thinking: 'How about a hat with a crest like a Peacock? A hat made, say, of Leopard skin, with a ridge of Eagle tail feathers – as a high crest. And maybe a long flap behind, like a Peacock's tail, to keep the sun off the back of my neck?'

Then he thought: 'That was a funny idea of Man's – the whole sky for a hat! With shooting stars.'

He chuckled. But then, abruptly, he sat bolt upright in bed.

A dazzling thought had just come to him. An inspiration!

He leapt out of bed. 'What a hat!' he cried. And he

ran through into his workshop. 'Quick, quick,' he gasped, 'before you forget it. Oh what a hat!' And he set to, there and then, making the hat of his dreams.

He did not notice how a tiny Bat swooped from the wall over his bed and followed him, flitting low over the floor, and flew up to hang again, upside down, under his worktable.

Camel was tramping across the skyline. He had decided the safest place for him was as far from God's scrapheap as he could get. As he ambled along the animals jeered at him:

'Hey, nose in the air, don't fall in a hole,' yelled a Coyote.

'Hey, galoshes, don't tread on your neck,' laughed the Gekko.

Camel just ambled on, pretending to watch the horizon. He had a funny walk. Each leg swung like a pendulum.

'Hey,' whistled a Canary. 'I need a bump on my back. Have you brought it?'

'Here he comes,' cheered the Baboon, 'with my new tail. Here comes the travelling heap of spare parts.'

'Have you brought my spare ribs?' asked the Leopard with a smile.

After a few hours of this, Camel thought of burying his head in the sand. The news had travelled fast and far. Even the Spiders in the thorn bushes knew what God thought of him.

'Maybe,' he was thinking, 'that is what it means,

being a mistake. There's no place for a mistake. And I'm a mistake.'

So he walked all night. And as dawn lit the sky he found he had come in a wide circle. He recognized the hill and God's workshop. He was right back where he'd started.

Then he saw an amazing thing. It seemed the Sun was rising on God's hill. But at once he saw it was not the Sun. It was something altogether peculiar. It was God in a hat. But what a hat!

And as the real Sun rose in the east, God's hat blazed out in the west. The birds didn't know which way to turn. The animals ran in circles. But then they all started running towards God.

His hat was astounding.

It was a great pale blue dome of turquoise. And moving up from the edge, from just above the middle of God's brow, was a huge, glowing ruby – like the red rising Sun.

The birds cried out, as if they could hardly bear it. The animals crowded to watch. As the real Sun rose in the east, and went behind a cloud, the dazzling ruby in God's hat rose higher, but instead of going behind a cloud it became brighter than ever, and golden. It had turned over. And now it was a huge round diamond, with gold behind it, so that it shone gold.

Man lowered his eyes and simply stood there trembling. Woman gazed and gazed, and her eyes filled with tears, as if to protect themselves from the dazzling fieriness of the hat.

And when all his creatures were gazing at him – and even Camel was gazing from behind a distant thorn bush – God took off his hat.

What he did then sent a cry of amazement through all his creatures. He turned the hat inside out!

And now that he put it back on his head, they could see that it was made of lapis lazuli, which is the rich, dark blue stone full of gold flecks like the night sky. And in this dark blue dome were studded all the Constellations of stars, as diamonds, emeralds and rubies, and a great Moon rose there made of tiny pearls.

Then God took the hat off again, punched it inside out, put it back on, and there was the blazing golden Sun again, climbing the turquoise dome.

'Which is best,' he asked Woman, 'to wear the day by day and the night by night? Or the day by night and the night by day? Which?'

But all she could say, in a trembling voice, was: 'Oh, God, what a hat! What a heavenly hat!'

At that moment a small black Bat appeared from nowhere. The Camel thought it was a big Bluefly. It landed on the hat and at the same moment became enormous. A Bat bigger than an Elephant wrenched off God's hat and flew upwards with it.

A roar of dismay went across the world.

God flailed his arms. Man and Woman stared up in terror.

'It's Frog-foot!' screamed Woman.

But God was quick. He hurled a thunderbolt. The Bat

dodged in the air as the bolt went smoking past. Another followed and just scorched the claws of his left foot. He changed direction and flew at the sea. The next thunderbolt sizzled past his ear and went into a cloud.

Immediately the cloud seemed to explode. It started to stab downward lightnings at him. Terrible electric shocks ran along the tips of his moustache and stood crackling there. His eyes went orange, then red.

With a yell he dropped the hat.

All the creatures saw the glorious hat tumble from the sky, and the splash that went up as it hit the sea.

None saw what had become of the Demon Bat. He had become a tiny Kingfisher, the size of a Sparrow, and he was already scooting along within inches of the sea, in the hollows of the waves, where not even God could see him. And so he got to land and vanished into a clump of bamboo.

God sat on the dunes weeping. He simply could not believe it. The Demon! All the animals and the birds cried under the trees and in the trees. Woman rested her head on God's wrist, to console him. Man sat at his feet, his head bowed.

Camel watched it all. If only Woman would console him, as she consoled God! Then, heaving a deep breath, he groaned a long, soft groan.

Woman made God some hot supper. Outside, the Sun was sinking to the edge of the world as a fiery red ball.

'At this moment,' sighed God, 'somewhere in the depths of the sea, the great diamond on my hat will have turned over, and the ruby will be glowing in its place, sinking towards the rim of the hat.' And he sighed again.

Then, a few minutes later, when the Sun had gone down and the full Moon was rising above the other side of the world, he said: 'And now my pearly Moon will be rising from the rim of the hat – but inside! All watched by the fishes. All in the bottom of the sea!' And he sighed again.

'What you need,' said Man, 'is some creature to go down there, and find it, and bring it back up.'

God looked at Man. Man had good ideas.

'Maybe some big fish could do it,' Man went on.

God shook his head.

'I didn't give them enough brains. If I had, they would have wanted to live on land. They'd have been unhappy in the sea. And I didn't want that.'

'Camel!' shouted Woman. She shouted in fright, because the Camel, still thinking about how Woman had comforted God, had just put his head in at the window.

God looked at Woman. What if she was right? Camel wasn't much good for anything else. But with a few slight changes he might be just the thing.

God leapt out through the door, and before Camel could get his long tangly legs swinging under him God had grabbed him.

'Not the scrapheap!' the Camel tried to groan. 'Please not the scrapheap!'

'You're the very thing we need,' said God.

The Demon raged in the bamboo thicket. He beat his own bald head.

'Idiot!' he snarled. 'Oh, idiot! You had it in your hands!'

But there was nothing he could do. He was a Fire Demon. If he had tried plunging into the sea, he would have been extinguished. He was so furious with himself, he returned to his wife deep inside the Red Mountains and told her everything. He wouldn't have cared if she'd swallowed him. He felt he deserved it.

But when she heard about the hat, her reply was strange. She took a nugget of iron ore in each fist. Her face contorted. Her bald scalp knotted into lumps, her dreadful eyes bulged, her mouth opened slowly, as she stared at her husband. And in her clenching fists the iron ore crumbled, fumes rose between her fingers and molten iron splashed on to the floor.

'Get me that haaaaaaat!' she screamed.

By the time the Demon flew up into the world, God was leading Camel to the sea's edge.

'Find my hat,' said God, 'and you will be first among animals. I will give you into Woman's care, and she will comb you and feed you. That is God's promise. Now go. And bring the hat into my hands.'

He slapped Camel's rump and the great beast set off, swinging his legs, towards the breakers of the sea.

God had made him able to walk under the sea. He had done this by making his hump hollow and filling it with compressed oxygen. At the same time, he had made Camel's bones very heavy, so he could not float. He could not even swim, with those bones. But he didn't need to. He now marched through the breakers and on down into the sea. As he marched across the sea bed it might have been dry land except for all the little fish that came to look at him.

God sat on the dunes, waiting. He watched a white sea bird, a Tern, circling and circling low over the sea. God smiled. 'That bird can't believe his eyes,' he thought. 'An animal walking across the sea bed. He simply can't believe it.'

God did not know that the Tern was the Demon.

And the Demon had a plan. He could see the Camel clearly, down through the green water. And the moment Camel found the hat, glowing on the bed of the sea, the Demon set off at top speed to Man's house. Man was out collecting food. The Demon worked fast. Woman sat in the garden, plaiting her hair so it could be tucked up under her hat. The Demon grabbed her, and when she opened her mouth to scream he jammed a big sponge into it. Then he tied her plait round her face like a gag and slinging her over his shoulder ran into the forest. But as he ran she kicked off one of her sandals.

Deep in the forest, he tied her wrists and ankles together with a creeper and pushed her down inside a hollow tree. He laid his ear to the tree trunk. 'Mmmmmmm,' it hummed, and 'Mmmmmmm,' like a hive of bees. Laughing, he ran back to Man's house, collecting her sandal on the way. He spilled water over a patch of the garden and trampled on it, leaving big froggy footprints. Then he flew up, as a Raven, carrying her sandal. Far below, he saw Man returning home. He dropped the sandal on to the path in front of him, then flew off, top speed, to the seaside, where he came down as a Tern, to sit bobbing on the waves, just beyond the breakers.

When Man saw the sandal, dropped by the bird, he feared the worst, and started to run. The froggy footprints were all he needed to see. He came howling to God at the seaside. God listened, jumped up, and the two ran off together.

A few minutes later, when Camel came marching up out of the sea with God's hat shining on his hump, he saw a figure waiting for him, on the dunes, where God had been.

'Where's God?' Camel tried to say. But the figure spoke:

'I am God's assistant. My name is Angel. Where have you been? God got tired of waiting. He's furious. I have to take you to him at once. Hurry!'

And he jumped on Camel's back and, sitting on top of the hat, directed him straight out into the desert towards the Red Mountains. Camel groaned and began to run.

All the rest of that day Camel went along at his best speed. After a few hours, they stopped at an oasis in the rocky desert. Camel was thirsty.

'Best be careful,' warned the Demon, who still had the shape of an Angel. 'The Demon lives in these water holes. He'll snatch the hat again if he finds us. We are carrying the Crown of Heaven, remember.'

And then, as Camel drank, the Demon snatched the hat off his hump and pushed him in. Camel sank straight to the bottom. It only took him half a minute to come walking out, but by that time, both Angel and hat had gone.

Camel ran round and round the water hole. He thought the Demon had pulled him in. 'And the Angel,' he thought, 'has gone to God to tell him that I have lost the hat.'

Inside the Red Mountains, the Demon's wife wears the hat. And the day of her kingdom is the day of the hat, when the diamond climbs over and down the dome of blue turquoise. And then she turns the hat inside out, and the night of the hat is the night of her kingdom. All her stolen plants and creatures are happier. But now that she has night and day, of a sort, she wants more and more of God's plants and creatures. So the Demon is busier than ever.

And out in the desert Camel wanders from oasis to oasis. He stares into the water holes. Sometimes he seems to see the hat on the bottom, with the moon and the stars. He can no longer walk down there under the water, because his compressed oxygen is long ago used up. Instead, he tries to drink the water hole dry. He fills the hump up with water. It's hopeless, of course. Then the hat seems to disappear, and he wanders along to the next water hole, groaning as he goes. And he stays out there, in the rocky desert, where he hopes, maybe, that he'll find the hat, in some small water hole, before God finds him.

The Grizzly Bear and the Human Child

When God created Woman he had to give her a toy.
While Man was away in the forest, collecting food, she
had to have something to play with.

God knew that she liked jewels. Jewels, gems and
precious stones of all kinds. Man had found her a few
of these and she would spend hours sorting them out,
arranging them and simply gazing at them.

So God thought: 'A living jewel would be just the
thing.'

That's when he invented Snake. How he made Snake
is another story. But when Snake was finished, she was
dazzling. Every scale was a different jewel. Best of all
were her eyes. Her eyes were such powerful jewels
they made God feel slightly funny when he looked at
them.

'My word!' he whispered to himself. 'What have I
done? I hope she's all right. But I must say, she's a
beauty.'

Snake lay there, looking at God. She felt very dark
and deep. She felt full of – full of – she wasn't quite sure
what. But she knew she ought to keep it hidden from
God, whatever it was. So she lay very still.

Woman was overjoyed with her new toy.

'You see,' God said, 'you hang it around your neck, and that's a necklace. Or she'll coil around your arm. And that's a bangle. Or around your waist, and that's a jewel belt. Or around your head, and she's a crown. Isn't she a beauty?

'And here's a little mirror to go with her. So you can see how beautiful she makes you look.'

Now Woman spent the whole day playing with her Snake. And Snake was very happy with their games. She would coil around Woman's neck, and rear up her neat little face beside Woman's face, and the two of them would gaze at themselves in the hand mirror.

'Oh, my beauty!' Woman would say. And she would actually kiss Snake's cold little nose.

Snake liked this. But what she liked best was Woman's warmth.

Man wasn't so sure about Snake. Those eyes made him uneasy. So he built Snake a hutch, under the floorboards, out of sight. From there, Snake could slide out into the garden. Or she could come up through a hole under the bed, to play with Woman. But when Man was at home, Snake had to be out of sight.

As he came home in the evening, Man would whistle a tune, to warn Snake. Then Woman would say: 'Oh dear, here he comes. Away you go. Sorry, my little beauty.'

And she would kiss Snake's cold nose. And Snake would slide away down, under the floorboards. And there she would lie, in the dark, listening to Man and Woman, and feeling left out.

One evening, Man brought home a Lamb. 'It's lost its mother,' he explained. 'Out there on the mountain, where life is tough. We shall have to look after it.'

So Woman looked after the Lamb. With Snake draped round her shoulders she would feed the Lamb milk from a bottle. And Snake would stare at the Lamb's furry little head, and its sleepy little eyes, as it drank.

Snake did not like this at all. Woman was too fond of this funny little thing. And once, when Woman suddenly snatched up the Lamb and kissed the top of its head, Snake went: 'Kssssssssssssssssssssssss!' And her forked tongue flickered in and out. She couldn't stop herself.

But the Lamb soon grew too big to cuddle. In fact, it very quickly turned into a Ram and galloped off to the mountain, where it looked for another Ram, so they could batter their heads together, which is what Rams love to do.

Snake felt happy again, coiled on Woman's warm stomach as she lay in the sun, or draped around her waist as she worked in the garden.

But then Man brought home a baby Rabbit – so tiny, it sat on his hand.

'Oh, he's lovely!' cried Woman.

And Snake, already under the floorboards, hissed: 'What now?' And she lifted her head so sharply she cracked it against the board above, and flopped flat for a moment, almost knocked out. That made her even angrier.

During the day, Woman played with the baby Rabbit and Snake had to pretend she liked it. Actually, she felt more like eating it.

'It would go down,' she thought, 'very smoothly. That would stop its idiotic little nose bobbing about.'

Instead, she did something amazing.

Woman was searching under her chest of drawers for the little Rabbit. She had left Snake coiled on her dressing table. Close to Snake's nose lay a comb. In the comb glistened two of Woman's hairs. A sudden thought came to Snake. She took the hairs between her lips and drew them out of the comb. Then, with a few twists, she coiled them around her head.

The next thing, Woman heard a strange voice – a woman's voice.

'Hi there!' it said.

Woman twisted around. There, leaning against her dressing table, was another Woman, almost exactly like herself and yet – different.

'Can I play too?' laughed the new one. And made three wild leaps across the room, turning a somersault and landing on her knees beside Woman.

'Where's this diddly Bun?' she cried, and raked her arm under the chest of drawers. 'Hey, here he is. Well I never!'

And she dragged the Rabbit out by its ears, squirming and kicking.

Woman simply stared at her new playmate.

'Who are you?' she gasped. 'Where are you from?'

'I'm Snake,' laughed the new one. 'Don't I look good? Come on, let's go have some fun in the woods. Find some more Rabbits maybe.'

From that moment, every day, Snake turned into another Woman, exactly like Woman. And all day they played together.

'But how are you so like me?' Woman kept saying. And Snake would answer: 'I am another you.' So that's what Woman called her: 'Otherme'.

'I like that,' cried Otherme and, flinging her arms around Woman, jumped into the river with her.

But every evening, as soon as they heard Man's whistling tune, Otherme turned back into Snake, and slid down her hole into the dark. Woman never breathed a word about her to Man. Otherme was a very exciting person, even if she was a Snake. And if Man knew about her – well, he might spoil things. He didn't seem to like Snake at all. Anyway, Woman didn't want to share Otherme, even with her husband.

Now and again, though, Woman remembered the baby Lamb and the baby Rabbit. Even while she was out with her new playmate, maybe swimming in the river, she would suddenly remember the Lamb. She would lie there, floating on her back, thinking about the Lamb. Thinking about the Lamb always gave her the strangest feeling. A very sweet feeling. And she thought about it more and more.

One night, when the Moon had risen over the forest,

Man and Woman lay in bed talking. And Snake lay under the floorboards, listening as usual.

'Aren't Lambs lovely,' Woman was saying. 'Isn't a Lamb the loveliest thing. Isn't it strange how it makes you want to cuddle it? I think it's the prettiest thing. It's just so pretty!'

'Very clever of God,' said Man, 'to think of the Lamb.'

'And the baby Rabbit,' said Woman. 'Why is it so pretty? Why does it make you want to cuddle it and kiss it?'

'Well,' said Man, 'it has a funny little round face. That's why. And funny little round ears. It's sweet, somehow.'

'Are all baby things like that?' Woman asked.

'Like what?' asked Man.

'Pretty,' said Woman. 'So you feel you want to cuddle them. And kiss them.'

Man was silent for a while. Under the floorboards Snake listened. At last Man said:

'Well, I suppose they are, come to think of it. Yes they are. Little birds. Even little pigs. Baby pigs are the sweetest things. Funny little faces.'

They were silent for a while. Snake listened to their thoughts working silently in the bed above.

Then Woman said: 'Would a baby of ours be like that?'

Another silence. But then Man said: 'I expect so. Yes, I suppose it would. In its way.'

After that, there was a long silence. Then Woman said: 'Will you ask God tomorrow?'

'What?' asked Man. 'Ask him what?'

'For one for us,' said Woman.

Snake slowly lifted her head. She listened hard. The house was so still she could almost hear the Moon. She thought Man had gone to sleep. But at last his voice came: 'OK, why not?'

Snake's eyes glared invisibly in the pitch black under the floorboards. They glared so hard they crackled. What was this? A baby Human Being? A new little playmate for Woman? First a Lamb. Then a Rabbit. And now this? Wasn't she, Snake, Woman's darling playmate? Wasn't she Woman's Otherme? Her living hoopla? Her adjustable jewel? So what was the need for a new little Human Being? With a funny round face and funny little ears?

Well, Snake would see about that! Snake would have something to say about that! Tense with cold fury, she slid along and out of her hole under the wall of the house, into the garden. Her eyes shone with dark power. A Frog's golden eyes were gazing at the Moon. Its body was wet with the dew. It did not know about Snake. But suddenly – it knew it could not move. An invisible power was gripping it. Then it was grabbed and swallowed. And it had no idea what had swallowed it. It simply went numb. Poor Frog!

Snake flicked her tongue. 'Tomorrow,' she hissed, 'we shall see. A baby Human? With a funny little face? A sweet little thing, with funny little ears? For Woman to play with and cuddle and kiss? Not if I can help it. Ksssssss! Ksssssssssssss!'

Again she raised her head and looked towards the house, so silent in the moonlight. A brainwave swept from the tip of her tail to the tip of her forked tongue in one shiver. She slid back under the foundation of the house and up through her hole into the room. Man and Woman were asleep, noses in the air. By the light of the Moon that came in through the window, Snake reared up and looked on to Woman's dressing table. There it lay, the necklace of tiny red seashells, like red finger-nails. She pushed her head through it and kinked her neck slightly so it hung there.

With the necklace swinging from her kinked neck, Snake poured herself back down through her hole, to her place under the floorboards, and there she curled up, waiting for day.

Next morning early Man kneeled in front of God, in God's workshop. He had made his request. And now he waited.

'Well,' said God. 'I hope you are quite sure you know what you're asking for.'

'Oh yes,' cried Man. 'We are, we certainly are. We've talked it over.'

God gazed down at the top of Man's bowed head. Well, it might be quite interesting, making a little Human. It would be a change, anyway, from what he was doing.

In the middle of his workshop stood an immense Grizzly Bear, on its hind legs like a Man. Its big round ears touched the ceiling. Its paws were raised, and nearly touched the ceiling. On each paw were five claws, each claw about six inches long and jet black. It was twice as tall as Man, with shaggy dark brown and gingery fur. All it needed was the breath of life. God was pleased with it. He didn't want to give it life straightaway. Once alive, it would be gone – out into the dark forest. No, he wanted to admire it for a while.

Just for a joke, he said to Man: 'You're sure your wife wouldn't prefer this fellow? He's all ready to go. She could have him now.' And he nodded towards the Grizzly Bear.

It was only now that Man saw what the huge dark shape was. And his eyes bulged. The Bear was so huge Man hadn't realized it was an animal. He had thought it might be a great rug, God's giant bedspread maybe, hanging to air. But now he looked at it –

'Ugh! Ugh! Ugh!'

Strange grunting noises came out of him and he began to shuffle backwards on his knees. As if the Bear had stepped towards him. He began to shake all over. He couldn't stop it.

'There,' said God, patting his head. 'Don't be scared. It's not alive. Here, take an apple. And tell your wife the baby's on its way. Off you go. Laugh. Be happy. Let me hear you laugh. How is your laugh these days?'

Man turned his bulging eyes and fixed them on God. His chin quivered.

'Go on,' cried God. 'Give us a good laugh. Come on, now – laugh!'

'Hahahahaha!' barked Man, and his eyes jerked

sideways back to the Bear. He thought his laugh might make it attack him.

'Forget the Bear,' cried God. 'Come on, a good old belly laugh. Like this: HAHAHAHAHAHAHA!'

God roared with happy laughter. The whole workshop shook and the door banged open.

'Come on,' cried God. 'Now: HAHAHAHAHAHA!'

And: 'HAHAHAHAHA!' roared Man, imitating God and trying not to look at the Bear.

'That's it,' cried God. 'Again!'

'HAHAHAHAHA!' roared Man. 'HAHAHAHA-HAHAHAHA!'

It was actually a dreadful sound. And as he tried to laugh, Man's eyes switched to and fro between God and the Bear.

'Let's hear you laughing like that all the way home,' cried God. 'Let's hear how happy you are with your news. The baby's due tonight!'

'HAHAHAHAHA!' roared Man, as he backed out of the door. 'HAHAHAHA! HAHAHAHAHA!'

He backed down the ladder, fell the last few rungs, stumbled across God's garden, glancing wildly backwards, and plunged into the jungle. Every moment he expected to see the Grizzly Bear burst out after him.

'HAHAHAHAHA! HAHAHAHA!' Laughing in that horrible way, he stumbled and fell, got up and fell again. Wrenching branches aside, falling over roots, he crashed through the undergrowth, laughing like a madman: 'HAHAHAHAHA! HAHAHAHAHA!'

'Remember,' God shouted after him, 'tonight.' He shook his head, smiling, and turned to his bench. 'Now let's see,' he murmured. 'A Human baby. Shouldn't take too long.'

God had almost finished. He was just fixing the last of the tiny perfect fingernails when the room darkened slightly. Somebody stood in the doorway. He looked up.

'Hello, Woman!' God smiled a broad smile. He gazed at her. She really did look pretty good. The big red flower in her hair perfumed his whole workshop. Her red shell necklace gleamed. He had never made anything else quite like Woman. And today she looked extra special. She looked so gorgeous, in fact, he felt – just a touch of fear. That surprised him. His hair prickled slightly, looking at her.

'Almost finished,' he said. 'How do you like it?' He pointed to the baby and his eyes danced, expecting to see her stunned with the sheer joy.

Instead she burst into tears. She stayed there in the doorway, her face buried in her hands, her shoulders sobbing.

'What's this?' God was amazed. 'What's the matter? Isn't it what you wanted?'

She shook her head so hard her red shell necklace clashed to and fro and tears scattered from her face like jewels.

'No,' she sobbed. 'No, it isn't.'

'But,' said God. 'But – but – but – but what do you want? Man said – '

Woman lifted her face. Her great eyes shone, her eyelashes glistening with tears. She stared at him. He could feel the power of her eyes gripping his.

'The Bear!' she wailed. 'I want the Bear! I don't want the baby I want the Bear! My husband didn't understand. The Bear! The Bear! Oh! Oh! I want him! Oh just look at him. He's all I want.'

'You want the Grizzly Bear?' God's voice squeaked. He could not believe it.

'Oh please! Please, God! Please! Please! The moment my husband told me about him I just knew. He's all I've ever wanted. I'm sorry – I'm sorry – Oh, please!'

And with a sobbing wail she seemed to fling herself back down the ladder, and lurched away over the garden, her arms writhing like scarves.

'Ooooh!' she wailed. 'Oooooh!'

God sat down. He truly was stunned. He shook his head slowly. He could still hear her wailing sobs as she ran through the forest. My, she was upset!

He looked at the baby on his bench. Then turned his head and looked at the tower of shaggy terror – Grizzly Bear, his great hooked paws lifted so high. He shook his head again, slowly. And slowly, he shrugged.

Halfway to Man's house, Woman staggered to a halt, panting. She leaned against a tree. She was still sobbing. But then – in the strangest way – her sobs became chuckles. Then laughs. She writhed her whole body and coiled into a loop, laughing. She stuffed the red flower into her mouth to gag her laughter, and the petals blew everywhere. She rolled full length among the orchids. At last she lay there, panting, lengthening, growing thinner. She gleamed like a Snake, and – she was Snake.

Snake!

Smiling, her head lifted, she slid homewards, the necklace swinging from a loop in the tip of her tail, and a petal sticking out of the corner of her long, curved mouth.

Man had made a little cradle cot. Woman had made coloured blankets. They sat on their bed, knees up, waiting.

'Did God say he would bring it himself?' Woman asked.

'Hard to say,' said Man, 'how it will come. I expect he'll bring it.'

Man played a little tune on his conch harp, which was a big seashell strung with twisted horse hairs. It was his latest song:

> ' "Come into my kitchen," said
>   The Spider to the Fly.
> "Nine sour apples
>   Make a Sweety-pie." '

Woman gazed at the window, the tops of the trees, the Sun going down red and clear.

'Maybe we should meet it halfway,' she suddenly said.

'Let me,' said Man. 'You stay. I'll see if he's coming.'

Man went out through the open door. Woman lay back on her pillow. She was trying to imagine what a Human baby would be like. Well, she supposed this was what it was to be happy. She listened to Man's little conch harp, plinkety-plonk, and his voice, so soft and peaceful:

> 'Said the Fly to the Spider:
> "Wrap me in a shawl.
> Oh I'll be the sweetest
> Baby of them all." '

But then she almost jumped out of her skin. A horrible scream – 'Aaaaaaaghghgh!' – out there in the garden. So horrible, she thought it must be some horrible new animal. Some hideous new giant bird, just made by God, as a mistake.

Man appeared in the doorway. His face was all mouth, and the scream came again – this time out of his face: 'Aaaaaaghghgh!'

He leapt on to the bed, grabbed Woman and fell with her over the other side of the bed. He rolled into the low space under the bed, bringing her with him, clinging to her tightly.

Now Woman heard a grunting roar. From under the bed, she could see something blocking the door- way of the house. Something was trying to get in, but was too big. It was jammed in the doorway, struggling to get through into the room. The house shook.

'It's the Bear,' gurgled Man. 'It's Grizzly Bear.'

She could see that its huge head, with its funny puffy

cheeks and big round woolly-looking ears, was through the doorway. But its shoulders were too broad, its whole body was too massive to get in.

'Look at its ears!' she whispered.

'Ears?' cried Man. 'Never mind its ears. Look at its mouth! And listen to it. And wait till you see its claws. Don't you know what horrible is?'

Its roar was weird, like a vast iron barrel bouncing down a rocky ravine. And deafening inside that room. Everything in there danced and trembled.

But Woman only cried: 'What's it saying? It's saying something. Listen! Listen!'

They both tried to listen.

'Stop your teeth chattering,' cried Woman, 'so we can listen.'

Man clamped his mouth tight shut. Yes, they could hear words, quite clearly, in that vast, shaggy bellow coming from the Bear's throat: 'Mamma! Mamma!'

'Oh no!' whimpered Man. 'I thought God was joking. He meant it. Oh no! I can't believe it! He's sent the Bear as your baby.'

'Dadda!' roared the Bear, ripping great splinters off the threshold with its claws. The doorposts bent inwards and cracked loudly.

'Mamma! Mamma!'

'That thing my baby?' cried Woman. 'Oh, please, God, no!' Then she too started to scream. She banged the floor with her fists then put her hands over her eyes. So there they were, Woman screaming with her hands over her eyes and Man sweating with fear, holding her, both jammed under the bed. While the house shook and jolted and the great Bear's terrible face twisted and pushed, and gaped and roared, in the doorway, trying to get in.

And under the floorboards, under the screaming and crying couple, Snake lay in the pitch darkness, on wood shavings, in a great loose knot, and smiled.

'How are things going?' said a big, familiar voice. At the same moment, the window was completely filled with a gigantic shining eye. It was God, peering in. 'Something wrong, eh?'

'Take him back!' screamed Woman. 'Take him back! He's too big! Take him back!'

God could see straightaway that things had gone awfully wrong. But what did they expect?

'Well,' he sighed, 'I really did think, you know, that Grizzly Bear might be a bit too much. But you would insist.'

His eye disappeared from the window and they heard his voice: 'Back there, Teddy! Come on, boy! Good boy! Come on, out of there.'

The doorway cracked again and the doorposts bent this time outwards as Grizzly Bear was pulled out backwards.

Woman crawled from under the bed and came to the door. She was fearless. Especially now God had arrived. She was also curious. God met her at the doorway. He handed her the Human baby wrapped in a giant orchid of speckled purple. She gave a gasp and clasped it tightly.

'Oh, God!' was all she could say. And now she was crying, but this time with joy not fear.

God smiled and turned to Grizzly Bear who was sitting in the middle of the garden.

Man came from under the bed and looked out over Woman's shoulders. The Sun had just set over the forest, behind the Bear. The red-gold rays coming through the tree tops from behind made him seem fringed with fire. His round ears were fringed with fire.

Woman was happy. She smiled happily at the Bear. It looked like a big fat dog, quite friendly. 'Look at his lovely ears,' she said. 'Aren't they sweet! Isn't he sweet!'

Man pushed his brows up crookedly and pulled his mouth crookedly down. He thought Grizzly Bear was pretty scary in any light. He could not forget his big shock, and what he had gone through under the bed.

'His ears are all right,' he said. 'It's the rest of him I'm not so sure about.'

God led Grizzly Bear into the forest, and Man and Woman watched them go, fringed with fire.

'I want one,' Woman said suddenly.

'What?' cried Man. 'What now?'

'A Bear,' she said.

He was afraid that's what she meant.

'No!' he shouted. 'No. No. No. Anything you like – but not that. I draw the line at a Bear.'

'Only a little one,' she said. 'It needn't be alive. Just a little cuddly friend for this one.'

She laid her baby in the cradle so she could look at it

there. Yes, there it actually was, moving its fingers.

Man did not want her going to ask God for a Bear. So he made one. A very small Bear. Nothing like God's Grizzly, of course. Just a baby-size furry Bear. For eyes it had lumps of amber. And round, woolly-looking ears. Woman sat this little Bear at the foot of her baby's cradle, looking at the baby.

'Here's Teddy,' she said. Her baby screwed up its mouth and blew a bubble.

Snake under the floorboards had not moved. Only, it no longer smiled. Its eyebrows had come down over its eyes in a hard, cross frown.

The Last of the Dinosaurs

In the early days, God made some strange creatures. New ideas were quite hard to find. When he thought up a Clam, for instance, he went on for ages – simply making different kinds of Clams, or things very like Clams, such as Mussels, Oysters, Razor Shells, and so on. And when he suddenly got the idea for a Worm he went wild – filling up the rivers and lakes and seas and lands with different kinds of Worm. It seemed he might never make anything else except Worms. But in the end he got bored and suddenly thought of Spiders.

When he thought of Dinosaurs he said: 'This is it. This is perfection. I'll never get a better idea.'

He stuck to Dinosaurs for an incredible number of years. And every day he thought up a new one. Actually, each new one was quite like the old ones, but he'd give it more horns, or a longer neck, or twice as much armour-plating, or make it five times as big. As he finished these creations, they lumbered out from under his hands, and ran on to the plains, heads up, looking for trouble.

God's Dinosaurs were all the same in one thing – they were a very fierce lot. They spent their time attacking each other and eating each other. The big ones ate the little ones. The little ones ate the big ones. The whole world was a battle of Dinosaurs. Wherever a Dinosaur looked, he saw Dinosaurs fleeing from him with squawks, or Dinosaurs rushing towards him with snarls. They were tirelessly fierce. And the noise was terrific. Every kind of cry, from twitterings like Swallows to screechings like Elephants. Some Dinosaurs were smaller than Swallows, and some were bigger than Elephants – even though they looked more or less alike, with their steely claws, their strong hind legs, and their horrible Dinosaur eyes.

Those were early days, and God did not know the world had become such a shocking place. He was too busy making new Dinosaurs to think about what the old ones were getting up to. All that interested him was 'my next Dinosaur'.

But he was finding it harder and harder to think up new ones. And one day he was stuck. He was making his latest model – but somehow it wouldn't come out right. He rolled it into a ball and started again. It still wouldn't come out right. He pounded it into a lump with his fist and started again. It still wouldn't come out right. He slapped it flat with his hand, sighed, laid his arm on his workbench and his head on his arm, and fell asleep.

He woke up almost at once – with a start. What had wakened him? He blinked, and started to model the clay again. Then he stopped.

A strange brown creature sat up in the middle of the

workshop floor, licking its chest. It was quite small, the size of a thrush. It had a round face, round eyes, round ears, a round belly, a round bum, and funny little hands. God reached down and picked it up. It was soft. Furry. It was the first furry thing God had ever felt.

'What are you?' he asked, and he looked at the creature with eyes as round and wondering as its own.

It looked back at him and wriggled its whiskers. 'I'm a kind of Bushbaby,' it said.

'Bushbaby?' God was very puzzled. 'What is that?'

'A baby from under a bush,' the creature replied.

'You came from under a bush?' asked God. 'Now tell me. Where did you come from, truly.'

'You dreamed me,' said the Bushbaby. 'In your bushy head.'

God scratched his chin.

'I know I never entered your thoughts,' Bushbaby went on, 'because you were so busy trying to think up horrible Dinosaurs. But you did dream me. So here I am.'

Yes, God remembered now. He'd dreamed of a green bush. And something had shaken the leaves. And out of the bush had crept – this very creature. He was fascinated.

A totally new idea! Soft, furry beings!

In no time at all, he stopped making Dinosaurs. Now he was on to soft furry creatures. All his Dinosaurs suddenly looked old-fashioned and stupid.

'What a waste of time,' he thought. 'I've made far too many.'

131

But then he saw what happened to his new creatures, in the world of the Dinosaurs. They didn't stand a chance. Those terrible steely killers, with their terrible speed, and their terrible jaws full of fangs, tore the soft furry beings to bits, or simply swallowed them whole.

God heard his new inventions crying at night in the trees, where they huddled together. But they weren't safe even in the highest trees. Speedy, small Dinosaurs, nimbler than any squirrel, came ripping up through the leaves – and with stunning screams threw them down to earth, where other Dinosaurs waited. Or flying Dinosaurs came cruising up, and with a grab and a flap snatched them away, eating them as they flew, like sandwiches.

God felt pity for his little furry ones. 'I've filled the Earth,' he thought, 'with monsters. I simply have to get rid of them. They'll have to go. I want the Earth to be safe, for my furry beings.'

So he set about wiping out his Dinosaurs.

A Demon from under the earth heard what was going on. He rose like a puff from a volcano, and appeared before God as a creature from outer space. God was quite pleased to see him. He asked for cosmic news, and the Demon invented some. Then the Demon came to the point.

'Now you're scrapping your Dinosaurs,' he said, 'we thought you might sell a few cheap. On our planet we have only fungus.'

'Too late,' said God. 'I doubt if there's one left. When I do a job, I'm thorough. Sorry about that.'

'If I find one, can I have it?' asked the Demon. 'There might be just the odd one left.'

'So long as I never see it again, it's yours,' said God. 'But you won't find one. I made my gaze deadly, and I let it rest on the valleys and the plains, and – poufff! – Nothing but fossils.'

'I'll just have a look round,' said the Demon, 'if that's all right.'

'Look in the caves,' shouted God after him.

The Demon was already speeding to the caves. And there in a deep tunnel, protected from God's deadly gaze, he found a Pterodactyl, still alive.

This Dinosaur had immense wings, a crocodile head, and terrible Dinosaur eyes that were mad with hunger.

'Is it safe yet up there?' asked the Dinosaur.

The Demon had brought him a Bushbaby. And as the Dinosaur gulped and swallowed, he told him that the happy days on Earth were finished. 'The moment God sees you,' he said, 'you are extinct. I'm afraid your day's past. But I can help you. I have a job for you.'

And so the Demon housed the Pterodactyl in a great cave, under a mountain. Each day he brought him a furry being, or a Snake, or a Lizard, to eat. And the Pterodactyl's job was to guard the Demon's gems. These gems were the Demon's only food.

The Demon was gathering all the gems in the world, and all the precious metal – the gold, the silver. He worked night and day, till the sweat trickled down his back and dripped off his stumpy tail.

He leaned against the wall. 'I have to get it all,' he explained to the Pterodactyl, 'before Man comes. Man will want it all, when he comes I shall have to fight him for every jewel. And, now that God's invented the Bushbaby, Man won't be long a-coming. Oh no, he's on his way right now. And when he comes – I shall need a guardian. I shall need you.'

'This Man you speak about,' said the Pterodactyl, 'will he be a sort of Bushbaby?'

'Bigger,' said the Demon. 'Meatier. And Woman, his mate, meatier still.'

The Pterodactyl's eyes did not change, as he smiled with his four-foot-long row of fangs. 'This,' he thought, 'is better than lying flat among the fossils.'

And pretty soon, Man arrived. And soon after him, Woman. On the third day, Man found a jewel. And when he gave it to Woman, she jerked her head back, and her mouth opened like a baby bird's: 'More,' she cried. 'More.'

A week later she found a little nugget of gold in a stream, where she was searching for pretty pebbles. She came to Man. 'This stuff,' she said, 'it's magic. Look at it.'

And when Man looked at the nugget of gold he felt the weirdest sensation. His palms were suddenly wet with sweat, a shiver crept up his back, his teeth ground together, and he gripped her wrist. He gripped it so tight that her fingertips swelled red as cherries. Then, very gently, with the finger and thumb of his other hand, he took the little lump of gold from her. And he gazed at it. It was shaped like a popcorn. And as he gazed, his brow tightened its wrinkles till it resembled a clenched fist, pressing down over his eyes, and his chin trembled.

'Where did you find this?' he whispered.

'It's mine,' she cried. 'Finders keepers.' And she snatched it back.

So they had their first fight. And when Man had won and had hidden the gold he told her: 'I only want to make it safe. Now let's find more, together.'

'Jewels too,' she said. 'You have the gold and I'll be quite happy with just the jewels. How about that?'

The Demon, sitting in a bush, smiled. He had worked hard and well. He knew the earth was almost empty of gold and gems. They were all in his cave, under the Pterodactyl.

He then slipped across to the hiding place, took the lump of gold, and ate it.

'Another puzzle for Man,' he laughed, and as he soared back to his cave he snatched a snake off a rock for his pet.

Man came to God and complained. There was no gold. There were no jewels. Or so little, it was making his wife sick. He needed the gold and jewels, yes and silver too, for her health. And what bit of gold he had found had vanished.

God couldn't understand it. 'The earth should be full

of those things,' he said. 'What's happened to them?'

When God asks a question, something has to answer. And now it was a snake, that stuck its head out of a hole in a tree and cried: 'The Demon collected the whole lot. The Demon's plundered the earth. It's all in his cave. Under the mountain. And he guards it with that horrible Pterodactyl that ate my mother and father.'

God's eyebrows rose. He had to laugh. So that's what the creature from outer space had been! And out of his laugh came a brainwave. He frowned, raised his right hand, and snapped his fingers.

In that second, all the gems, all the lumps of gold and silver in the Demon's cave, melted. Like a colossal heap of snow.

And they flowed out into the rivers of the world as streams of fishes. Every kind of fish was created there, in that flashing snap of the fingers. The Pterodactyl floundered and screeched, then flapped up on to a cave ledge. The Demon stared. Then he understood.

His cry shattered that mountain. And out of his cry came a burst of magic power. He changed the Pterodactyl into a bird no bigger than a Goose. The long neck was still there, and the long mouth. But the bird had feathers, and strange long legs.

'Go wade in the rivers,' the Demon shouted. 'Save my treasures. Find my treasures. Go, go.'

The Pterodactyl bird flapped up out of the cave and sailed over the rivers of the Earth. Everywhere under the windy ripples he saw the glimmerings of the fish, the glints and flashings as they turned.

'Gather them,' yelled the Demon, flying above him. 'You stay as you are till you've gathered them all.'

So there he is. But how can he gather them all? He wades along the edges of rivers, peering down. Now and again he jabs. And now and again he does come up with something. But it's never a jewel, never a lump of gold or silver. It is bright, maybe. But it is never anything but a fish. So he swallows it.

And sometimes, remembering his happier days, he grabs a Lizard. Or a Snake. Or even a Water Rat. And he swallows it. Man has called him Heron.

And when he flies up, with his broken-looking, ponderous wings, and lets out his cry, his awful scrarking gark, he reminds you of a Pterodactyl. And when you see him close up, and get a good look at his terrible little eye, you know, for certain, he is one.

The Secret of Man's Wife

Once again, God had dreamed a startling dream. And once again, when he woke, he'd forgotten it. What was it? He sat at his workbench, staring at a knot in one of his floorboards. Something dazzling had appeared in his sleep. Something to do with Man.

He was still puzzling, trying to coax his dream back, when he realized that somebody was standing in the open doorway of his workshop. He looked up and saw Man, wearing the most woebegone expression.

God took a deep breath. Another complaint! When would Man come to him without a complaint? But he shot up his eyebrows, smiled with delight, and cried: 'Man! How are the carrots coming on?'

Man licked his lips. He lifted his face for a second and God felt a little pang of pity as he glimpsed the awful toiling difficulties behind the brown eyes. Then Man's gaze sank again to the floor, as if the weight of his troubles were too great to hold up.

'What's the matter?' cried God. 'Has something been digging them out?'

'It's not the carrots,' said Man. 'They're fine. It's my wife again.'

God nodded. 'Hmm!' and waited. Now, he thought, here comes the complaint.

'She's restless,' said Man.

God waited.

'In fact,' Man went on, 'she's become altogether – peculiar.'

God raised his eyebrows. He was always interested to hear about his creations. They were full of surprises.

'So what's new?' he asked, in an easy voice, reaching for a bit of clay. 'How is she peculiar?'

'Can you explain,' asked Man, 'why she is always looking past me?'

God frowned, and rolled the clay between his thumb and forefinger.

'She's always looking towards the forest,' said Man, 'as if she were expecting – somebody. She leans on the doorpost and stares – at the forest. She's always sort of – waiting.'

God waited.

'Then,' said Man, 'when I'm doing something, repairing my sandals or carving a new paddle, I feel this weird, chilly feeling, and I look up and – she's watching me. She's not looking at me in a normal way. She's watching me, out of her eye-corners, with a look that – . A very strange look. As if I were – I can't explain it. And the moment I see it and ask her what's the matter she gets up and goes out. She goes off some-where. Into the forest.'

God stroked his beard.

'What does she do there?' he wondered aloud.

'I think,' said Man, 'she meets somebody. And she laughs – she has this laugh. It's not a happy laugh. A completely peculiar laugh. She laughs, showing all her teeth – then starts somersaulting all over the garden. Then she starts crying. She sits there sobbing.'

God frowned. This certainly was pretty strange.

'Who do you think she meets in the forest?' he asked.

Man stared at him. 'I think,' he said, 'I think she meets your wolf.'

God stood up and slapped his hands together, flattening the clay into a leaf.

'What an idea!' he cried. 'What makes you think that? That's a crazy idea.'

But Man went on, still staring at God, so that God did just wonder, for a second, whether Man had gone a wee bit crazy.

'I keep getting this feeling,' he said, 'that my wife wants to be a Wolf.'

Now it was God's turn to stare. He was stuck for words. 'Wants to be a Wolf?' It did sound crazy.

'Nearly every night,' cried Man, 'I dream she's a Wolf running in the forest. Or she's a Wolf with its forepaws on my bed, staring down at me. And I wake up, and do you know what?'

God was almost afraid of what he was going to hear.

'She's pacing up and down the room panting. And I'll swear, in the dark, her tongue's hanging out.'

'No!' shouted God. 'You're dreaming it.'

Man paused for a while, his lips clamped.

'And then,' he added, 'there's a smell.'

God's brows twisted two or three different ways at once. What now?

'It's actually quite an exciting smell,' Man went on. 'But it's – not exactly doggy, not exactly – '

They both became silent, staring at each other. God sat down.

'Well, what can we do about it?' said God at last. 'What do you want?'

'I've thought about it,' said Man.

'What have you thought?'

'If you,' said Man, 'can extract from her whatever it is, whatever this wolfy thing is, that makes her so peculiar, maybe we could have that as a whole separate – animal. A sort of pet, maybe. Or maybe just let it run wild. And that would leave my wife as she used to be. As you made her. Nice and normal.'

'Ha!' God laughed and slapped his knee. 'Well,' he thought, 'who knows? Who knows what peculiar sort of creature will come out of her, if what Man says is true?'

'Maybe I'll watch her awhile for myself,' said God. 'Then decide.'

So God began to watch Woman. And it was just as Man had said. She had become peculiar. Locking herself in Man's cupboard, laughing and weeping. And at the full Moon she did more than pace the floor, she ran out into the forest – letting out short, awful laughs, more like shrieks than laughs. She would come home next morning worn out, scratched, muddy, and sleep for a whole day.

At other times, especially at the new Moon, she would pace about Man's house, almost running, occasionally turning a few somersaults, or breaking into a wild whirling dance, where she seemed to have several extra legs and arms, doing the most amazing tricks – like dancing for minutes on end, her arms and legs spinning round in one blur, on top of a tiny stool, or bounding round the room from wall to wall without touching the floor, or scampering about the garden arched backwards with her face between her thighs at fantastic speed.

God shook his head. He was baffled. Maybe Man's idea was the solution. But whatever the crazy thing inside Woman was, how was he going to get it out?

He went to ask his old mother's advice. As he told her about Woman she seemed almost to go to sleep. She sat in her corner, her funny long hands folded over her head and her head bowed. When he'd finished, he thought she really had dozed off. But suddenly she said: 'It sounds like a Demon.'

God gave a start. A Demon? He was always forgetting about the Demons.

'A Demon's got into her,' his mother said again. 'Or, if not a Demon, something very like a Demon.'

'So what's to be done?' asked God. He felt quite helpless. 'Can't we get it out, whatever it is?' And he sat there wondering just what kind of Demon. Some sort of fly? Or worm? Demons can take any form.

Then, speaking very slowly, his mother explained what had to be done . . .

'. . . and that's your only hope,' she said when she'd finished. 'And it might go wrong.'

God went to find Woman. Instead, he found Man, stretched out on his bed, looking pale and ill. Man stared dully at God. 'She's gone off again,' he said.

'What happened this time?' asked God.

'Nothing,' said Man. 'I only said: "I love the black hairs on your legs." You know, you gave her a few sort of wispy dark hairs on her legs.'

God nodded.

'And she let out a terrible wail,' said Man. 'As if I'd reminded her of something dreadful. And she ran off into the forest. It's getting me down, God.'

'Today,' said God, 'we're going to fix this.' And he set off into the forest.

He followed her deep tracks in the soft jungle soil. She'd been running, her heels had made deep holes. Soon they came to harder ground and God had to use his sharp eyes. Suddenly he knew he was being followed. He slipped behind a great clump of lilies. And who should come along, bent double, inspecting his tracks, but Woman.

'What a nice surprise!' he cried, stepping out in front of her – but she had already fainted.

He carried her to his workshop and sat her in a chair. Her head lolled, her limbs flopped. 'Wake up,' he whispered, patting her cheeks. But she was still out cold.

He stood scratching his head. What could he do if she wouldn't wake up? He felt painfully sorry for her as she slumped there, with her long eyelashes closed, her plump little mouth slightly open. Could his mother be right about her? Could she really be possessed by a Demon? His favourite among all his creations? She looked so delicate and pretty.

Just then his mother came in.

'Well,' she cried, 'aren't you getting on with it?'

God pointed at Woman. 'Shhh!' he whispered. 'She fainted. I scared her.'

'Ha!' crowed his mother. 'Fainted? A likely tale! You don't know the tricks of these Demons. Anyway, that's good. It makes it easier. Tie her to the chair.'

Woman stirred and moaned softly.

'Quick!' his mother almost screeched. 'Before she wakes up.'

God tied Woman's limp arms and legs to the chair.

'And a rope tight round her waist, tight to the chair,' cried his mother.

God did that too.

'And a gag,' cried his mother, and she gave him her own scarf. God tied the scarf round Woman's mouth, gagging her.

'Now where's the clay?' asked his mother. 'We've got to have the clay.'

God brought out a lump of clay, nicely soft, about the size of a pillow. He thumped it and kneaded it and shaped it roughly into a ball.

'Put that on the floor in front of her,' ordered his mother. God did as he was told.

Woman had opened her eyes. She stared wildly at God's mother. She knew about God – but God's mother – Man had never mentioned God's mother. She tried to cry out: 'What are you going to do to me?' but only managed to gurgle. When she realized she couldn't speak, she was more frightened than ever.

'Stoke up the furnace,' cried God's mother. God began to shove logs into the great glowing doorway of the furnace at the back of his workshop. Woman rolled her eyes towards the jumping flames.

'Build up a good big blaze,' shouted his mother as the flames crackled into a roar. 'We want to get her red-hot through and through. The heat can't be too fierce. White-hot would be best.'

Woman now rolled her eyes towards God's mother, trying to make them scream for help. But God's mother bent over her only to say: 'Are you wearing any jewels, my dear? If you are, we might as well have them. The flames will ruin them and that would be a pity.'

Woman's eyes went dry with horror. She stared again at the flames, then at God's mother, and gurgled. She twisted in the ropes. Her toes and fingers writhed. But God's knots were good.

'Bring out the anvil,' cried God's mother, 'so we've lots of room to swing the hammers.'

God lifted the massive iron anvil out into the middle of the room, and leaned the two long-handled smith's hammers against it. His mother took hold of one of them and made a practice swing. She was immensely old, but that didn't make any difference to her power. As she whirled the hammer everything in the workshop seemed to flinch. When the hammer hit the anvil, Woman's head bounced as her chair jolted, and a spark stung her knee.

Woman had now closed her eyes and tears poured over her cheeks into her gag. Were these two actually going to shove her into the furnace and make her red-hot and then pound her with those hammers, as if she were a horseshoe? She tried to faint again but she couldn't.

God and his mother were inspecting the ball of clay.

'It should do,' his mother said, poking it. 'You see, there has to be somewhere, some bolt hole, for her good Angel to go. We don't want to hurt that, do we? So we make a hole in the clay, here, then her good Angel can dive into it out of harm's way.'

God made a hole in the clay, pushing his fist into the middle of the ball.

'That's enough,' said his mother. 'I've done this before. As we slide her head-first into the furnace, and as the flames get a really good grip on her, her good Angel will come whizzing out. You won't see it. But it will dive into that clay. There it will be absolutely safe. Then we'll simply roast her old body to a crusty crisp in the flames and pound it to dust with our hammers. And that will be the end of the mischief. It's quite easy. You can wet the dust and make fresh clay for something else afterwards.'

Woman's eyes seemed to want to leap out of her head and through the window. Her hair stuck out on end all round her face. Then she stared at the clay ball. At the dark hole in the clay ball. Then at the raging and throbbing glare of the furnace's open door. Then at the anvil. Then back at the lump of clay and the dark hole in it.

God was saying: 'And I suppose I can just remake Woman out of this ball of clay, with her good Angel inside it.'

'Clever boy!' crowed his mother. 'You've got it. It's all quite simple. Right. Now. Are you ready?'

And she fixed her great round hungry eyes on Woman with a savage glare, like a frightful Eagle. 'Into the flames with her!' she screeched, and God picked up the chair with Woman tied to it. He raised it over his head and took a step towards the furnace.

At that moment the ball of clay gave a thump and wobbled. God paused and looked at it. His mother looked at it.

Sure enough, it was squirming, like a sack with somebody inside.

In one great leap, God's mother pounced on the clay and with one smack of her hand closed the hole.

'Now,' she cried, 'quick. Get a shape on to this.'

God set down the chair, hoisted the clay on to his workbench and began pummelling at it, pulling at it, tweaking it, pressing it, gouging it with his thumbs. He went at it non-stop, as if he were battling in a dark room with an invisible assailant. And at last he had it. And there it was. He held it up in his two hands, at arm's length, and laughed as it bunched and kicked and twisted.

It was a strange beast. And, true enough, it looked quite wolfish. But it was red – nearly the colour of the furnace flames. And its throat, and its belly, were white – even whiter than Woman's face, who lay there in her gag and her ropes, her eyes closed, once again in a dead faint.

Its slender legs were black, black as the wispy hair on Woman's shins. Its eyes were amber. And as it writhed, it seemed to laugh, and its fangs were white and curved like tiny new moons.

Suddenly it twisted right out of God's hands, hit the floor, bounced in one streak out through the door and was gone.

God's mother laughed a cackling sort of laugh, wiping her hands on her apron. Then she gently undid the gag from Woman's mouth and untied the ropes.

'Take her home,' she said. 'She'll need a good sleep now. We scared it right out of her.'

'So that was the Demon?' asked God, as he picked up Woman in his arms.

'That,' said his mother, 'was not quite a Demon. I'm not sure what it was. But it was very pretty.'

'Well,' said God, 'it looked to me like what I'd call a Fox.'

After that, Woman was a new person. A few days later, Man came to her very excited. 'I've seen a new beast,' he told her. 'A dazzling new beast. God really is getting better all the time. I met it on the path. It was so gorgeous I asked it to come home and live with us and be a pet.'

Woman pretended to be surprised as he described its red fur, its amber eyes, its slender, jet-black legs, its blazing white chest and chin and its miraculous lovely tail.

'And wouldn't it come?' she asked. 'Did it reply?'

She really did feel quite curious to know the answer.

'It replied,' said Man. 'It was very polite. It said: "O Man, O husband of glorious and beautiful Woman, it is the fear of being anyone's pet that has turned the tip of my tail quite white." And it showed me the tip of its tail. And, do you know, it was perfectly white.'

'What a pity!' said Woman, but she smiled to herself.

She never told Man what she had gone through in God's workshop. And God never told him either. So Man never knew the Fox had ever had anything to do with her.

But one day in his orchard he heard a soft clapping, behind his raspberry canes. Creeping close, he saw an incredible sight. His wife sat there, clapping her hands lightly, while the Fox danced round her on its hind legs, leaping and twirling, its wonderful tail floating round it like a veil, its silvery tongue hanging and its teeth flashing in its long smile. He was so astounded he simply walked right up to them crying: 'Wonderful!' But before he had finished the word, the Fox had vanished. In a flash, it was nowhere to be seen. Where had it gone? How could it disappear so completely, so quickly? Man blinked. Had he been seeing and hearing things? Woman stood up and yawned. She came towards him, smiling sleepily as if he'd wakened her up from a nap.

And Man felt so mystified that he said nothing. All he did was gaze at her, smiling slightly, frowning slightly. He simply did not know what to make of it.